Our Future Good

Ross Books
PO Box 4340
Berkeley, California 94704
ISBN 978-0-89496-121-2 (paper)
ISBN 978-0-89496-122-9 (e-Book)
ISBN 978-0-89496-075-8 (Audio Book)

(Ghost) Riders In The Sky (A Cowboy Legend)
By Stan Jones
(c) 1949 (Renewed) EDWIN H. MORRIS & COMPANY, A Division of MPL Music Publishing, Inc.
All Rights Reserved
Reprinted with Permission of Hal Leonard Corporation

Library of Congress Cataloging-in-Publication Data

Kirby, T. J.

Our Future Good / by T.J. Kirby.

    pages cm

    ISBN 978-0-89496-121-2 (pbk.)
    ISBN 978-0-89496-122-9 (e-Book)
    ISBN 978-0-89496-075-8 (Audio Book)

    1. Evolution--Fiction. 2. Science fiction. I. Title.

    PS3611.I737F88 2013

    813'.6--dc23

    2013025899

Our Future Good

By T.J. Kirby

Ross Books
P.O. Box 4340
Berkeley, Ca 94704
www.rossbooks.com
www.OurFutureGood.com

Table of Contents

Chapter 1

Our Future Good

The African plains were never quiet, especially in the middle of a summer night, but the noises were all in the distance and Mary didn't feel threatened by them. She looked up from her bed and stared at the unbelievable night sky. There were countless stars shining very brightly because there were no city lights to wash them out. The Milky Way astounded her! She relaxed and enjoyed the clear moonless night, as a perfect warm breeze blew gently over her body.

There was something about the whole experience that was very primordial and made her feel, deep down in her bones, that this was where we all came from and where we all belonged. She sighed, wishing she could stay there forever, but she heard the sound of flutes and French horns playing an energetic wake-up song. Suddenly the whole African experience transformed to sunrise on the plains because it was really just a very high-resolution video being displayed on the dome of Mary's bedroom in Aipotu, California.

Mary did one of those really long great-to-be-alive stretches in her bed. The bed was made of FormGel, a jelly-like body-temperature substance that conformed perfectly to your body so there were no pressure points to make you uncomfortable.

She'd heard that a long time ago people used something called bed sheets and blankets on their beds, but the household temperature was so perfect now that there was no need for such things. Last night, she'd worn an experimental NutriSuit to bed, and she smoothed her hand down the long, rippling, body-stocking type garment with a smile. *It worked!*

She smiled and popped out of bed, full of energy and eager to start the day.

Mary was at her boyfriend Joe Davis' home. It had been nice of Ken and Alice, Joe's parents, to let her stay over and wait for him. He was due back early this morning, but there would not be much time to sit around because Mary and Joe were going to their first Project Day today. They had both just turned eighteen, so now they would be given a chance to decide what project they first wanted to work on as adults. This was a major day in their lives, and she was brimming with excitement, wondering what sort of choices they'd be given and what they'd ultimately choose. She worried about Joe because she wanted to work with him but he was attracted to a dangerous journalist project.

Mary started taking off the NutriSuit as she walked toward the wall of the dome at the foot of her bed. Just before she reached the wall, a double door zoomed open to reveal a very modern bathroom. The spa-like room was covered with a floor-to-ceiling seamless granite-like surface heated to a perfect body temperature. The surface could change color and even display images, depending on your mood or desire.

Mary chose *Ancient Roman Bath*. The bathroom formed a

large walk-in whirlpool tub, in keeping with the Roman theme. As she was lowering herself into the steaming tub, a soft computer voice said, *"Joe Davis calling, Joe Davis calling."*

"Hi, Joe!" Mary said excitedly. "Where are you?"

"Hey, pretty lady!" came Joe's clear voice from speakers all over the room.

She grinned, thinking about something she'd learned in history class. Years ago, believe it or not, people used to hold a piece of plastic up to their ear to talk to someone. That was one of the first things to go as soon as what historians were starting to call "The Computer Conversion Age" got underway. When you think about it, there was no reason a phone couldn't hear you just as clearly as any other human could hear you. Nowadays, phones were designed to whisper to your ear if you wanted a private conversation through a speaker hidden in your earring or lapel.

"Joe, I just did my first night in a NutriSuit and it was fantastic!" Mary said. "I gotta tell you about it!"

"OK," said Joe. "I'm almost home. I should be there in fifteen minutes. I'm running a little late, but we should be able to make Project Day on time."

"Great!" said Mary. "I'll see you soon."

She finished bathing and hurriedly dressed, then made her way down the hall.

The Davis' house was pretty common. It was all one level, flat to the ground, and it stretched out over 4,000 square feet with a big backyard. The home had a master dome with hallways connecting to smaller dome rooms to the left and right. You could have an endless series of rooms off the hallway if you wanted, used for bedrooms or entertainment, and the whole ceiling surface area of any dome in any room could be used as a display if you wished.

Mary found Joe's mom, Alice, in the main dome. A good section of the main dome wall was playing the news and Alice glanced at it as she walked by. She suddenly stopped, because the news was about the International Space Station, commonly referred to as ISS, and another similar station called L5Pilgrim, which people sometimes referred to as L5P.

"The friction," the announcer said, *"between ISS and L5P has now moved to the boiling point. There are even some people who say ISS should physically invade L5P and take over the station. We now have a summary from our journalist, Bruno Nightfire."*

"Oh no," said Alice, giving Mary a worried look as she entered the room. "I gotta stop Joe from getting more involved in this!"

"I am sorry to say," Bruno Nightfire reported, *"that L5Pilgrim has been experimenting in a very unauthorized way with their inhabitants. Something has to be done to stop things before it is too late."*

"Hopefully he'll choose something different." Mary gave Joe's mom a sympathetic look. Joe liked journalism and was deeply into covering this story, but there was a lot of danger if he decided to go after it. Mary was also hoping that Joe stayed away from the L5Pilgrim issue, but for a far more selfish reason. She couldn't bear the thought of the two of them being on separate projects, and she had her heart set on working with NutriSuits.

Through an automatic sliding door, Mary could see out into the backyard, where Joe's little brother, Bobby, was watching excitedly as some workers completed his KiddieDome, which was beside the pool, right next to Alice's PlayDome, which she used for arts and crafts.

"Is it Bobby's first day of lessons?" Mary asked, to distract Alice from her obvious worry.

Alice smiled and nodded, going to the door to wave at the little boy. "Yes, he just turned four. I can't believe how quickly he's growing up."

Just then Joe drove up. Electric cars are silent, but Joe was loudly broadcasting one of the hit songs they both loved and Mary smiled. "Joe's here!" She ran outside just as Joe got out of the vehicle, and she threw herself in his arms.

Cars, of course, had stopped having drivers long ago and this had influenced the shape of the car, because when you change the way a tool functions, you generally changed the form of the tool as well.

Joe's car was about the size of what they used to call a SUV. However the top of the car was an arc – a semi-circle starting at the nose of the car and going over the top and down to the rear bumper. Basically, it was a dome on wheels. All cars were like that and people affectionately called them Bub-bleVans.

Joe laughed and caught her up in his arms, spinning her around and then kissing her.

When he put her down, Mary saw that Alice had come outside as well.

"Alice," Mary said, "I did my first night with the experi-mental NutriSuit, and it was super! I can't wait to hear from everyone else! Joe and I are going to Project Day now and you gotta come!"

Alice smiled with the loving but lonely smile of a mother

who knows her child is almost ready to leave the nest and go out into the world.

"That's really great, Mary," Alice replied. "I will call Ken a little later and maybe we can make it in time for the speech and walk through. By the way, Joe, I just saw that Bruno Nightfire guy on the news and the whole conflict between the ISS and L5P space stations is really heating up. You're not going to get in the middle of that, are you?"

"I don't know if there is any way for me to get there," Joe answered, obviously disappointed. "They are shutting down communications with L5P, but it is a critical story and I will talk to Sam, my journalism teacher."

Alice bit her lip, looking nervous, but didn't comment any further. "Well, you two have fun at your first active Project Day."

"Sure, Alice," Mary said offhandedly, anxious to be off. They were already running late. "Thanks for letting me stay here last night. We never would have made it in time if Joe had to go all the way to my house to pick me up."

"You're welcome," Alice replied as she moved forward to give Joe a hug and a kiss on the cheek. "Pick wisely," Mary heard her whisper to her son before she moved away.

"See you soon," Joe told his mom. Then he grabbed Mary's hand and pulled her toward the BubbleVan. They had to get to Project Day. Their future awaited.

* * *

Alice watched Joe and Mary drive away, feeling sad that her baby was all grown up, yet happy for him as well. Mary was a nice girl, and she was happy he had found her. Perhaps she could talk him out of going to the space station. Mary was so excited about the NutriSuits that Alice was reasonably certain she'd talk Joe into choosing that project, which would be far safer.

She walked through the house and out to the KiddieDome, which had just been completed. She couldn't believe that Joe was choosing his first project the same day that Bobby started his lessons.

"They're done, Mommy," Bobby squealed as she approached. "Can I start my lessons now?"

"Of course," Alice replied, taking her young son inside the KiddieDome and getting him set up. Once the computer-animated teaching program began, Alice walked a few feet away to her Play Dome, which was furnished with a table and a very comfortable stool with a tall back made of FormGel.

As she sat down, she could look over to her right and see into Bobby's KiddieDome and hear the computer-animated character saying, "That's great! Now how much is $1 + 4 + 5$?"

As soon as Alice had entered her PlayDome, Brandenberg Concerto number three, with strings and French horns, began to play, one of her favorites because it was so positive and upbeat.

While the music ran muted in the background, a rectangular area of the wall about three meters long and two meters tall lit up. Though she was reasonably certain Joe would choose the NutriSuit project, she wanted to keep up with the news from the space station anyway. The volume was low, but she could make out two local politicians arguing over how to expand the city.

"If we give the developers permission to build a bridge," said one politician, *"it will open up a whole lot of space for them to develop homes."*

"Yeah," said the other politician, *"but you and I both know that home developers already have a huge project going with a dozen Renovators busy at work right now. I say don't allow the bridge for now, so the developers will clean up more of the old city. Tell them they can do the bridge once the old town is cleaned up."*

Alice walked over and sat on the high stool at the table.

"Would you like to pick up on the last artwork you were working on?" the computer asked.

"Yes," Alice said absently, still keeping half her attention on the news and worrying about Joe. The table lit up and a hand-blown glass sculpture with rainbow streaks of color appeared to be floating in mid-air.

She put her hands out over the table so that she could "grab" the object and sculpt it with her hands, just like you used to sculpt with clay. She made the neck of the object a little taller. It was easy to move the object around, because the computer knew where your hands were. There was a painter's palate of colors to her right and Alice touched a deep peacock blue. Then she touched the art work and painted a blue stripe on it.

An annoying commercial for WorkerBots came on. Fortunately, the sound was turned way down so it did not bother Alice very much. For a long time, she let herself become lost in her art.

She knew quite some time had passed when Bobby wandered out of his KiddieDome and walked into her PlayDome.

"Mommy," said Bobby. "What are you doing? What were you making?"

Absorbed in her work, but happy to have her son around, Alice kept her eyes on her artwork.

"I am making an *object d'art*, dear," she said.

Bobby was getting a little antsy now. He'd obviously come over to get some attention and felt he was not getting enough. He began hopping up and down in place with his hands clasped in front of him. "What's an objects dart, Mommy?" Bobby asked. "What's that, Mommy?"

Alice smiled and hurried to finish up. She'd never be able to concentrate now that Bobby was here. "It's just something nice and pretty, sweetie. Don't you think this is pretty?"

Completely uninterested, Bobby began jumping up and down, doing jumping jacks. "Look at me, Mommy! Look at me! Look at what I am! Look at what I am!"

Alice held her left hand up to the wall.

"Done – make a copy," she said and a nearby replicator machine started grinding out a sculpture of her artwork.

Alice turned to Bobby with a very loving smile. "OK, tell me, sweetie, what are you? Tell me what you are."

Bobby had accomplished the monumental task of getting his mother's attention but had not yet figured out what to do once he got it.

He held his hands over his head to keep her attention and started turning around and around in a stationary circle while his brain whirled at a hundred miles an hour, trying to come up with something.

"I am....I am... I am....I am..."

Bobby suddenly stopped turning. He had finally hit on something! He held his hands apart and up in the air for a touchdown and hopped up and down. "I am our future good, Mommy. I am our future good. I am our future good."

Alice went down on her knees and hugged and kissed him. "That's right, sweetie, you are the future good of our society," she replied, knowing he must have heard the term during one of his lessons. "Now let's talk about what that means. You are going to do more lessons, right?"

Bobby nodded his head up and down.

"So you will do General Lessons," said Alice, "like math and science and lots of other subjects. You will do most of them at home, so you can move quickly through the lessons, but there are some, like science experiments and especially social time, for which you will need to go to school. School will be lots of fun. There will be Subject Events where you will talk to other kids about what you learned and you will work as a team to do some assignments. As you go along, you will be taking tests at home and school. Then there will be a big day like today. After you are older and have passed lots of tests like your brother has, and you have finished your General Lessons, then you are ready to do projects and you get to go to your first active Project Day where you will choose a project to go join."

Bobby was sort of listening, so Alice continued, "Do you know that Mary and Joe are going to their first active Project Day at school today? On Project Day, everybody picks a project to do. You can switch projects any time you want to, but most people that want to change projects wait until Project Day, which comes twice a year, to find their new project to work on."

Bobby was now in automatic nodding mode, looking very content.

"At the start of your first project," Alice continued, "and for the rest of your life, the government will automatically put a little money into your bank account each week. It is what we call a Technology Dividend."

Alice kind of rolled her eyes, thinking about how to explain it. "You see, sweetie, it is not a lot of money. You could probably live on it, if you really wanted to, and some people do, but almost nobody does. Life would be too boring for you if you just sat around doing nothing, so you will join a project somewhere and make more money. You can even start your own business or project, which lots of people do."

Alice brushed Bobby's hair back and kissed his forehead. Bobby obviously loved every second of her attention. If he was a cat, he would be purring.

"Now tell me, Bobby," said Alice. "Why do we go to school? What do we do there?"

"Dance and play and speriment," said Bobby with a self-satisfied smile.

"That's right," Alice said. "We learn to dance with other kids and play sports and you get to experiment with science in the labs. So schools are our most important meeting place, where you can get together with other people. You make friends at school and you can even do some lessons together, if you want to."

"Mommy," said Bobby, looking suddenly concerned and grabbing her leg. "I am going to stay real close to you, Mommy. Can you go to school too, Mommy?"

"Yes, sweetie," said Alice, "anybody can go to school anytime in their life and everyone does. School is almost like what they used to call a country club but with lots of classrooms and labs attached. Once you have done your first Project Day, you have to pay a little money each month to go to school, but it is a very small amount. You could even pay it out of your Technology Dividend and still have enough money to live on. People go to school all through their whole life and they love it. It is a great place to meet other people, get together with friends and learn about the latest technology or just to do lessons, artwork and socialize."

"Mommy, where's Daddy?" Bobby suddenly asked, growing tired of the subject of school.

Alice grinned. "He's at work. Should we call him?"

Bobby nodded excitedly, and Alice pulled a cigar-shaped cell phone from a thin tubular pocket by her armpit. On each shoulder, Mary had a lapel with a shiny black object that looked like a black marble cut in half. This was her 360-degree camera, which worked with her cell phone and most people called a SavvyCam. The SavvyCam was not only a camera. At the base of the half-marble shaped SavvyCam were tiny speakers. So as you walked around, you could be filming a 3D version of what you saw. Some people liked to wear their SavvyCams as earrings so the speakers could "whisper" your phone calls into your ears.

Alice held the base of the tublar-shaped cell phone and pulled it up like an antenna on an old car. As she held the base and pulled the top, it expanded to a rod about one meter tall. She then grabbed the side of the rod and pulled out a rolled-up screen. That was why people used to call these ScrollPhones when they first came out. She could make the screen whatever size she wanted.

While doing this, she said, "Phone, call Ken."

Eventually the screen was one meter tall and one meter wide, light as a feather and very thin. Ken's voice came over the speakers. "Hi, Alice."

"Hi, sweetie," said Alice. "Open your phone so Bobby can see you."

For a moment there were the sounds of a lot of shuffling on Ken's end. Then Ken appeared on the screen with a straight face, which immediately turned into a big smile when he saw his son and wife in real time.

"Hey, Bobby!" said Ken. "How are you doing, buddy?"

Bobby clapped his hands excitedly. "Daddy! Hi, Daddy! Where are you, Daddy? You need to come home, Daddy. You need to come home *now*, Daddy."

"I will be home later, son. How is your day going, babe?"

"Ken, I am feeling strange. It's the first active Project Day for Joe and Mary. I can't believe my baby is leaving home so quickly. It feels like he was born just yesterday!"

"I know, babe," said Ken. "Things go by so quickly."

"I am worried, Ken," Alice admitted. "What if he picks a stupid project and he gets sucked into something he really regrets spending his time on, like a Renovator? I am even more terrified that he is going to get into journalism and get involved in politics like the ISS versus L5P issue. Ken, let's go to Project Day and see if we can steer him in the right direction."

"OK," said Ken. "I don't really have to be here today. Why don't I just come home now and we can go to Project Day? We can bring Bobby along for fun. I'll see you soon. I love you."

"I love you too, dear," said Alice.

"I love you, Daddy!" said Bobby, making sure he was not outdone.

"I love you too, son," Ken said with a grin.

Chapter 2

Driving to Project Day

The inside of Joe's BubbleVan was pretty common. The vans were designed to allow people a lot of creative layouts for the seats, which could be easily slid around the floor and then anchored in any position you liked. Joe's van had the standard two rows of seats, which could either face each other for socializing, or be pushed back to back so each occupant could have their own screen. They could also be pushed together to make a sofa-like seat.

Mary and Joe preferred to configure the van's seat like a sofa, so they could cuddle together, talk and make out.

"I'm sorry," Joe said as the BubbleVan pulled away from the house. "I have been lending the van out and running it night and day forever without a charge, so I have to make one quick stop to change the battery."

"That's all right," Mary assured him, though she was a little annoyed. They were already running late. Changing your battery was so quick, he should have found time to do it earlier in the week, so that they weren't late to Project Day. Didn't he realize how important this was?

After a short drive, they came to the service station, which was basically a tunnel that looked like an old-time car wash. Joe guided the BubbleVan on to the conveyer belt, and confirmed his identity with the service station's computer.

"*ID confirmed,*" the computer said. "*The battery swap will take about three minutes. Your new battery is insured until your next swap. We will check your emergency battery too. Thank you for using our service and please have a wonderful day.*"

"This whole thing is just killing me!" Joe exclaimed as they waited for the battery to be changed. "I thought I had it all figured out. I thought the most important thing to get involved in was the NutriSuit project with you, but now this L5Pilgrim thing blew up in the news, and I really feel it is a major event. I happen to know Sam, who is in charge of the Journalism department here on earth for ISS, and he told me he is getting really worried. This Bruno Nightfire guy is acting as spokesperson for ISS, and he is also in charge of security. That's not good, because he is strongly against the L5Pilgrim community, yet he is acting like he is an impartial journalist. Nobody really gets to talk to the people at L5P, and there must be a million people at the station."

Mary frowned. She wanted to support Joe, but she also really wanted him to work on the NutriSuit program with her. "So are you thinking of doing a journalism program?" she asked neutrally.

"Nobody knows me, and I have no project work record, so Sam feels he might be able to get me into L5P to report on what is happening there. I feel I gotta go there, understand it, and report on it. Sweetie, why don't you go to space and do this project with me? I love you."

"Joe," Mary pleaded. "You know I love you too, but you also know how much I want to do the NutriSuit program. We've been talking about this for months." She gave him the I-am-not-moving-and-if-you-want-some-more-of-me-you-better-change-your-mind kind of look meant to crush any further argument. "I just did my first night with my NutriSuit and it was a real thrill. This is where all the excitement is! Think about what we can do!"

"Oh, man," said Joe, still looking unconvinced. "I want to work on the same project with you. I really do, but this is a really big thing for me!"

She smiled at him seductively and decided to try another tactic. Wrapping her arms around his neck, she started kissing him passionately. "Just think about what you'll be missing if you don't stay on the same project as me," she whispered.

"Good argument," he admitted, kissing her in return and pressing her back on the sofa.

"*Joe Davis, your battery swap is complete,*" the computer said, interrupting them.

With a groan, Joe moved away and gave Mary one last lingering kiss. "I guess we need to get going."

Like the dome rooms at home, the entire dome inside the BubbleVan was a screen. As they started back toward the school, Joe's mom popped up on part of the screen.

"Joe, sweetie," Alice said. "Your dad and I are going to go to Project Day, and we're bringing Bobby too. I am dying to see what the latest projects are. So don't be shocked if you bump into us, and I hope you don't sign up for one of those

Renovators."

"OK, great, Mom," Joe said with little enthusiasm. "Maybe we will see you."

"Hope to see you, Alice," Mary said, trying to be nice and friendly. She really did like Joe's family.

"I hope we don't bump into them," Joe admitted after his mother signed off. "We have some important decisions to make, and I don't want my mom in the middle of it. She'll be all teary-eyed and worried about me."

Mary hugged him, suddenly realizing that Joe was more important to her than the NutriSuit program was. After all, they had the rest of their lives to do different projects. She could always work on the NutriSuit project later. She was used to Joe bending over backward to make her happy so maybe it was time for her to start doing the same for him.

"OK," she told him with a coaxing smile. "Go ahead and try to convince me why L5Pilgrim is so much more important than the NutriSuit project."

Joe gave her an appreciative smile, his eyes lighting up with happiness at her sudden interest. "Watch this horrible excuse for journalism," he said. "Car, play L5Pilgrim summary."

Channel 2 News came on the screen and blasted the headline, *ISS to Vote No to a New Human Species!*

"Behind me," the reporter said, looking at a video in space, *"you see the dark black outline of the L5Pilgrim community, which is at the core of this great controversy. Bruno Nightfire at ISS has reported to us that the rebellious station has been creating a whole new species of humans with possible disastrous consequences for us all. Living at L5P will transmute your body in a way that can never be corrected. Fortunately*

for us, Bruno and his security team at ISS have introduced leg-
islation to the ISS board of directors to have ISS take over L5P.
Dylan Thomas is the elected leader of L5 Pilgrim, and he is the
only person who can commit the rebellious station to reversing
its disastrous course. Unfortunately, Dylan Thomas refuses to
come forward and discuss these issues with anyone. Instead he
has reduced all visitations and communications to the station
to almost zero in recent months. Fortunately, we are some-
times able to make limited contact with Amy Worthington, who
we regard as kind of a spokesperson for the community. We
will try to get her now....”

The screen fizzled a bit, but then sharped to a clear picture.
The landscape of a hill, with green grass and a rolling val-
ley, appeared with some mountains in the distance. The words
L5Pilgrim Portal showed at the bottom of the screen.

Mary heard some girlish giggling and bantering, and then
suddenly a lovely young blonde woman popped onto the
screen, along with a flapping sound. She was suspended in air,
because the people at L5Pilgrim had apparently chosen to live
at almost zero gravity. She was smiling broadly and looked
extremely pleased and excited.

“Thank you, Amy, for agreeing to speak to us today,” the
reporter said.

“Oh, no problem,” Amy replied. *“I am happy to do it.”*

“I know you can’t be here in studio, because your body has
been so badly transmuted that you can never return to Earth.
My question is, why are you allowing Dylan Thomas to do this
to your people? Don’t you have concern for the people whose
lives you are destroying?”

Mary frowned at the reporter’s question. That was rather
rude and condescending. Amy certainly didn’t look like her

life was being destroyed. In fact, she looked far happier than anyone Mary knew.

Amy only smiled though, not seeming to take offense. *"No, we love it here! You should come and join us! Here you go – spread the word!"*

Amy slapped an almost transparent sticker on the camera lens. The nice green valley was still visible, but now the L5Pilgrim logo floated in the air above it. Amy ducked off screen. The transmission held for a few seconds then fizzled a little bit and went black.

"Did you see that?" Joe asked, gazing at Mary with heated intensity. "That's horrible. Everybody knows what a journalist is supposed to do. A journalist is the foundation of a democracy. They are supposed to deliver the news by presenting both sides of an issue clearly and in depth. Then everyone gets to discuss the issue and decide what to do. All that guy is interested in doing is promoting the political cause headed by Bruno."

Mary frowned. "I understand why you're so concerned, but why do you think you need to be the one who fixes it? Surely there are plenty of other people who could go there and do a more unbiased job of reporting the situation."

"No one else seems to care," Joe explained in frustration. "Somebody's got to do it. In fact, I'm calling Sam right now. Car, call Sam."

Mary leaned back in her chair, folding her arms as she stared at her boyfriend in dismay. *Man, he is really passionate about this.* She started to wonder if he'd already made up his mind.

In fairly short order, Sam came on the screen. He was short, older, probably near fifty, with a shiny bald head and a pragmatic expression. "Hi, Joe," he said. "Have you decided whether or not you're going to L5Pilgram yet?"

Joe shot Mary a guilty look. "Not yet. In fact, I'm still trying to figure that out. Are there any new developments?"

Sam nodded. "I've become increasingly worried about Bruno. He is not only in charge of security on ISS, but he has put himself in a position of being the chief news outlet for ISS. It is a real bad conflict of interest. I would like to replace him and put in a new independent journalist. I was your teacher for your Journalism Lesson, and I know you can do a good job, but I can't remove Bruno because he is too powerful, and I can't yet prove he is doing anything wrong. I have found out that he was a founding member of the Avatar Initiative, which you might have heard about."

"Yeah," Joe said, looking at Mary. "That is the almost religious-like movement that wants to create robots that look identical to humans and then get humans to transfer all their thoughts into the robot. They got so whacked out on the idea that a dozen of them thought they had transferred their souls into the robots and then committed suicide. Crazy, crazy!"

Mary shuddered at the thought of a bunch of crazy people thinking they could live forever in robot bodies. Why would you even want to?

"Yeah," said Sam. "I can't prove it, but Bruno was one of the founding members. Just before the suicides, he pretended he left the group but he actually talks to them all the time. I think he wants to take over L5P and make it a giant home for Avatar Initiative followers. All I can do is complain to the board, which I have done, but that is not going to stop his desire to take over and close down L5P. To make things worse, L5P was part of the expansion of ISS before they broke away, so all the communication feeds for L5P run through ISS, and we are getting little to no contact with them. What little contact we have has to be approved by Bruno. I am working on a fix to this so I can access the L5P portal directly, but it will take a day or two. If I can get you into L5P, then I can access your SavvyCam as you go around L5P and get a direct video feed. Then all you have to do is interview Dylan Thomas. There could be lives lost if we don't act real quick because accelerating L5P back to normal gravity could cause biological issues we can't control or predict. The fate of L5P will rest on what Dylan Thomas has to say. Who knows, perhaps they need to be shut down and brought back under control. Anyhow, I am not sure if I can get you into L5P or not but I will know shortly. If it does happen, you will need to leave right away."

"OK," Joe said, fairly humming with excitement. "Keep me informed."

Sam nodded and signed off.

"Well," said Mary, a little overwhelmed by everything she had heard during the last few minutes. She hadn't really realized that so many people's lives were at stake. As much as she liked the idea of working on the NutriSuits, that didn't sound nearly as exciting or meaningful as what Joe was working on. "There is nothing you can do unless Sam can get you into L5P. So let's just see what happens at Project Day. We'll make a decision once we know all the facts."

"Does this mean you're actually considering going with me?" Joe asked hopefully.

Mary laughed and threw herself at Joe, knocking him back on the sofa, and started kissing him again.

When they finally came up for air, she grinned. "Well, I wouldn't say that I've made up my mind yet either. But I like that you're so passionate about this. It shows me that you are really going to do some amazing things with your life, and letting all those people have a voice on a world stage so we hear their own thoughts about what is going on at L5P might be a good place to start."

"Thank you," he told her fervently, starting to kiss her again.

She laughed and broke away. "Well, just promise me that you'll keep an open mind about the things I'm drawn to today, and I promise you that I'll do the same. Deal?"

"Deal," Joe agreed happily.

Chapter 3

Project Day

Project Day was held in a huge, dome-shaped building. All the way around the inside of the dome were a ring of smaller domes, assigned to each local school. The headmasters would give all the graduating students a pep talk and then simultaneously turn them loose in the larger dome, which was basically a huge convention hall packed with Project Administers from many different businesses.

Any business with projects that needed to get done could send representatives to Project Day, and they would set up booths to try and attract the workers they needed. Of course, most jobs were done by WorkerBots, but there was always the need for humans to oversee the projects and monitor the WorkerBots.

Project Days were held twice a year, and were the perfect way for businesses to connect with both new graduates with the latest knowledge, anyone else who had completed whatever project they'd been previously assigned to, or people who just wanted to try something new. There were also funders there, who would invest in you if you wanted to start a business.

The dome Mary and Joe's school had been assigned to was furnished very comfortably, with a thick rug, the perfect temperature, and extremely comfortable FormGel chairs that contoured to your body. The atmosphere resembled a giant living room party where everyone was family. People sprawled comfortably all over the place, in the chairs and also just stretching out on the floor. There was a wonderful sense of informality to these events, a time for celebration, not stiff pomp and circumstance.

"Thank you for coming to Project Day, whether you are here just to look or make an active decision for your life," the headmaster said with great enthusiasm. "If this is your first time to an active Project Day where you actually join a project, then congratulations! You have passed all the General Lessons and you are ready to join a project. This is going to be one of the most exciting and important days of your life. You have spent a long time in school and you have passed enough lessons so that you are now ready to put all that knowledge to use. We all know why we have Project Day – to join or start a project!

Very faint upbeat music was playing in the background and the dome started to fill with pictures and animation to dramatize his points.

"You were born at a time of tremendous change and challenges. Let's just consider a few of the challenges before us." Clips of NutriSuits began to flicker across the screens, and Mary gripped Joe's arm in excitement. She hoped the headmaster gave a good presentation of her favorite project, something that would convince Joe that he should choose NutriSuits instead of Journalism.

"Hundreds of thousands of years ago, humans would whack a plant or animal to death, perhaps they would singe it over a fire and then they would stuff it in their mouth. That is how we provided nutrients to our bodies. I don't have to tell you that until very recently we had not made much progress. We were just using our body like a giant garbage disposal. We stuffed food in our mouth and let our body try to grind up whatever we consumed. What happened is exactly what you would expect to happen. All the junk that was in our food clogged up our veins and eventually caused our body to grind to a halt and die. How tragic! How incredibly Neanderthal! We can do better than that! It is a natural part of the evolution of humans to want to find a better and cleaner way to give our bodies the nutrients they need. There are a lot of projects that are deeply involved in advanced ways of nitrating the human body."

Mary clapped enthusiastically, but Joe still seemed distracted, not really paying attention to the headmaster's speech at all.

"The world of robots, or, bots as most people say, is also tremendously exciting," the headmaster continued, and the images on the screens switched to various scenes involving robotic technology. "We have WorkerBots, FixItBots, Helo-Bots, and countless other specialized bots. A long time ago, the computer industry was progressing rapidly in understanding human speech and creating robotic arms to lift and work with materials. Somewhere along the line, some of the major car manufacturers woke up and realized that they could mount all this computer gear on a strong dune-buggy type vehicle.

The result was the first wave of WorkerBots that could do chores like construction, window cleaning and maintenance of large buildings and even gardening. From there, the industry exploded and the first mover companies captured most of the market. Today, WorkerBots are invaluable to us. We have Fix-ItBots creating and repairing other bots so you can order up a whole army of bots if you have a big job to do. The industry is ever expanding and always in need of help."

Another spattered round of applause swept through the room, and Mary noted with consternation that Joe clapped louder about bots than he had about the NutriSuits. She began to realize she was never going to win him over to her cause.

"Replicators are another really great project to join." Once again, the screens changed scenes, this time to Replicators at work making things like clothes and human body parts. "Where would we be without our Replicators? As we all know, this revolution in technology started long ago when the first 3D printers were made. They were able to create parts like a gear or wheel or axle. They quickly evolved to the point where they could not only make the wheels, gears and axles but they could assemble them and output a little red wagon. From there on, the industry exploded to what it is today. At the same time this was occurring, 3D printing of human body parts were developed. I don't have to tell you that there are tremendous challenges and excitement in developing this industry further. You will never be bored if you join this great project."

The headmaster leaned forward on the podium, his gaze intense. "Another great project is to work on various social issues. For example, a big issue is the controversy regarding the use of nanobots and artificial organs. Now that we have the potential technology to extend life to unheard-of degrees, the question becomes, should we? With all the artificial items we pollute our bodies with, you have to ask the question — are we changing the human body and brain so drastically that our souls are at risk? What is the human soul? Where do you draw the line between human and machine?" He paused for a moment as he let all this sink in.

"And you," he pointed his finger around at the crowd, "are the generation who will decide what path we take and what we will evolve into."

As the headmaster continued his speech, Mary spotted Alice, Ken and Bobby. As soon as Bobby spotted Joe, he ran recklessly through the crowd and jumped into Joe's arms, hugging him tightly. Joe laughed and kissed Bobby on the forehead.

This was clearly not going to be Bobby's kind of event. Anything that took more than 90 seconds was too long. He immediately started asking random questions, making it difficult for Mary to hear the headmaster's speech.

The music grew a little more dramatic.

"Here is another very exciting project – Space Rangers!" the headmaster proclaimed. "As many of you have probably heard, there are thousands of asteroids and rocks floating around in space. We are just now trying to put in place an asteroid intervention program where we identify hazardous asteroids and go out and intercept them. It is an exciting and very rewarding project to be involved in."

Close up images of actual Space Rangers putting rockets on asteroids to nudge them away from Earth filled the screen along with images of outposts on other planets.

"Space Rangers," the headmaster continued, "are also the

first to respond to space ships that find themselves in distress. They also provide support for scientific research on other planets. Space Rangers are the backbone of human exploration and development of outer space – they really go where no one has gone before and see things humans have never seen."

By now the screens were full of scenes of the exploration of Europa and the development of Mars.

"You can do your first work for various companies, getting involved in journalism or operating a Renovator – there are an endless number of things you can do to get your first experience and you can move from project to project. You can even work for the LS or MS political parties."

Bobby started pulling on Joe's arm. "Joe, what's a MS? What's a LS? What is it, Joe?"

Joe grinned at Mary and then leaned over and whispered in Bobby's ear. "Bobby, we have to be real quiet so people can hear. I am going to tell you what is happening, but we have to whisper so nobody hears us."

Bobby nodded and stared at Joe expectantly.

"We have journalists who tell us the news," Joe told Bobby in an undertone as the headmaster droned on. "We also have two political parties who discuss the issues in the news. One party has people who feel we need to have more government control or More Socialism – that is the MS party. The LS party feels we need Less Socialism or government control so they are the LS party. We make sure both parties have real good speakers so the public understands the pros and cons about any big decision we have to make. Then we vote for the politicians that will best represent us on the issues."

None of this made much sense to Bobby, but he obviously

loved the idea of whispering secret information back and forth.

"Whose side is the journalist on?" Bobby said.

Mary giggled when she heard this.

Joe rolled his eyes. "That's always a big problem. The LS and MS parties grade the major journalists from the news services as to how fairly they presented their party once a month, and you can see the scores the journalists got every time they deliver the news. Not only is the score there but there is a link you can click on to see why, in the words of the party, the journalist got the score they did. So what happens is that people will not listen to news shows with bad scores and they favor news shows with good scores. This means the shows with low scores, or bad journalism, will get much less advertising money. Every month, the news journalists are graded again so they can improve their scores. If you hire real bad journalists all the time, you will eventually run out of advertising money and go out of business."

Mary knew Bobby had no clue what Joe was talking about, but she thought it was cute that Joe had the patience to try and explain it to him, and she was interested to hear his simplified take on something that was obviously so important to him.

"OK everybody," the headmaster suddenly exclaimed. "Let's go see all the exciting projects you can choose from!"

A huge timer on the wall hit zero and all the doors to the room rolled back, exposing the center of the huge building. Thousands of students and their families all poured into it at the same time from all the schools. The center floor was jammed wall-to-wall with booths from hundreds of companies, big and small. Every company was vying to get the best workers, and they hawked their products like barkers at a carnival.

As Mary, Joe, his parents and Bobby started walking through the dome, Mary was a little overwhelmed by all the people shouting and trying to get her attention.

"No artificial wombless births!" proclaimed a wild-eyed man at the fringe of the crowd.

"Renovate the nation!" shouted another man from the Renovator booth, which was huge with a monster display.

"Robotize the world!" yelled another woman, gesturing to a display so large, it had its own section with lots of small booths. Robot technology had gone crazy and people were robotizing almost any chore a human had.

The Dogs-R-Us booth was a classic example. Videos and demonstrations showed miniature dune-buggy looking robotic devices that chased after dogs over almost any terrain. When the dog stopped to poop, the machine immediately ran up and cleaned up the mess, so no more doggie bags were needed when walking a dog in a city. Mary knew most homes had a docking tunnel where robots such as these and other robots such as lawn mowers could dock and clean themselves.

Small robots moved around the floor in a crazy dance. They knew where the other robots were so they also weaved around each other. In real life, there were not that many dog robots running around the streets because there were not that many people walking their dogs. You could also have a robot follow you around to carry things, but it was becoming increasingly unnecessary because there was not that much to carry around with the improvements in the Replicators.

Then there was the whole world of FixItRobots or FixMeRobots. Almost every household had different kinds of worker robots that went around the house doing whatever chores you had such as cleaning surfaces, building maintenance and gardening. FixItBots were the robots that repair these robots. It was a quickly growing business and people at these projects were especially aggressive at trying to get the attention of passersby. Mary had a headache by the time they managed to run that gauntlet.

Mary grabbed Joe's arm and tugged him toward where she wanted to go. "Let's go see TransDermal. They are doing just what I want to do."

Mary knew deep down that she was not going to convince him, because he seemed almost religiously devoted to his desire to visit L5Pilgrim and tell their story, but she wasn't going to give up without a fight.

The TransDermal booth was not far away. Joe rolled his eyes, but allowed Mary to drag him over to it.

"Mary!" yelled Susan, a woman who had been trying to recruit Mary for TransDermal for some time now. "I'm so glad to see you."

"I used my suit last night and it was really great!" Mary exclaimed as she hugged Susan.

"I'm so glad you liked it," Susan replied, sizing up Joe, who was scanning the crowd, obviously looking for the Journalist Project.

Mary had already explained to Susan that she would not join the TransDermal Project unless Joe did too, so Susan was prepared to do her best to recruit him.

Susan grabbed a NutriSuit off her table and shoved it at Joe's chest, making him look at her. "Oh wow, Joe, this is just your size. I am sure you are going to love it!"

Joe looked like a swimmer starting to be dragged out to sea by the tide, and Mary could tell he was scrambling to think of a way to get away from Susan without seeming rude. "Fantastic, Susan! Let me take it home and Mary and I will get back to you."

Susan obviously sensed she was losing the deal. Mary looked at her hopelessly, silently begging her to try harder.

"How about a quick look at what we are doing?" Susan said, while trying to walk backward and drift them over to the booth.

"Hey, Mary!" Joe interrupted. "I just saw the booth I was looking for. Let's make a quick trip over there. Susan, I promise you we will be back to you on this in the morning." Joe began to pull Mary away, which annoyed her somewhat. Their deal was that he was at least supposed to listen to the Trans-Dermal pitch.

"OK, I look forward to hearing from you. Don't forget me!" Susan said helplessly as Mary and Joe disappeared into the crowd.

Mary quickly realized that Joe really hadn't seen the Journalism booth, from the random way he pulled her through the crowd. She didn't know whether to be furious or just laugh. He was so set in his desired project that she didn't know why she'd even tried. She also has to admit that she found his passion and dedication pretty sexy. She was not nearly as passionate about NutriSuits as Joe was about journalism and started to resign herself to the fact that they'd be going to L5P

At last, Joe spotted the Journalism Project's booth and dragged Mary there determinedly.

"Sam! I finally made it to Project Day!" said Joe. "This is Mary."

"Hi, Sam," Mary replied. "So you're the one who is trying

to take Joe away from me." She was only half-joking.

"Don't worry," Sam said, obviously sensing her concern. "Joe said he will never leave you, but I'm sure you know by now that he has some things he has to get out of his system. Have you considered going with him?"

Mary nodded in exasperation. "Yeah. We've talked about it."

"That's good," Sam said, relief coloring his voice. "Because I talked to my contact and we have someone who can get you into L5P. If Joe covers the story, I can get it on the air and it will be big national news."

Joe perked up like someone just electrocuted him. "Done deal!"

"I don't know. Let's talk about it tonight." Mary was determined not to let anyone talk them into anything before they'd had a chance to discuss it. Picking a project was a big deal and it was something they were going to have to live with for quite awhile.

"OK," said Sam. "Talk about it tonight and let me know quickly because this guy is only there for a little while longer. If you don't want it, I have to find someone else fast. You can call me late tonight, if you want to."

Mary and Joe eventually left Project Day. They just sat in each other's arms for a while during the ride home. They had to make a decision tonight but it was so heavy they just wanted to talk about something else.

They knew they loved each other so they started talking about where they wanted to live. One obvious option was daisy chaining onto Joe's parents' house, which was done a lot. Joe brought up the architectural plans for the house. They talked about whether they should add on or just get a new home from one of the Renovator Projects. They couldn't decide, and it had been a long day. Their car pulled up at home, they got out, and then the car went by itself to the garage, where it would get serviced by robots.

As they entered the house, they could hear Bobby, screaming, almost in tears. Apparently he broke the head off his toy horse.

"Mommy," he cried, trying to get Alice's attention. "Look at this. Look at this, Mommy. It broke! Fix it, Mommy!"

"Oh, sweetie," Alice said. "I am so sorry it broke. Just get a new one. Put it in the Replicator, sweetie. Go ahead. You can do it."

Bobby pouted for a minute or two and finally decided he was not going to get much more attention so he dragged the horse over to the Replicator. A large door opened and Bobby pushed the pieces into the machine. The door closed.

"Replicator, new toy," Bobby said.

The Replicator knew from the ID tag what the item was. It then started grinding away, making a new toy while it disintegrated the old toy and recycled the material.

Mary grinned at Bobby as he pulled his new toy out of the Replicator moments later and scampered away with it.

Alice looked up at them, smiling a bit nervously. "Joe, sweetie, where have you decided to go? I hope is it not to some dangerous place. You are not going to work on a Renovator, are you?"

Joe shrugged uncomfortably. Alice was a well-meaning but nagging mom and that was the last thing Joe needed right now. "I haven't decided yet, Mom. Mary and I are going to go talk about that right now."

"You're not going to work on a Renovator, are you?" Alice repeated, unwilling to let him go that easy. She gave Mary a look that made Mary feel like Alice thought her own opinion of her son's future should trump Mary's. "I hope that Sam guy did not talk you into anything crazy. There are a lot of politics in that L5Pilgirm confrontation and people can really get hurt. That is outer space, you know, and all kinds of weird things are happening on that rebel station. That's not good for anybody…."

Joe politely slow-walked past his mom toward his room.

"I know you are concerned, Mom, but I have to sort this out. Let me think it over with Mary and we will decide tonight for sure." Joe pretended to be exhausted, so he did not have to listen to his mom anymore and Mary followed him to his room.

Once they arrived in Joe's room, Joe activated their sexy jungle scene and the music they usually made love to, but Mary didn't jump him like usual. They had too much to talk about, and she wasn't going to let him off that easily.

"Room, ocean scene," she said, giving him a piercing look. The music changed to soft, soothing tempo and the jungle theme disappeared, replaced by a beach at sunset, the waves lapping at the shore in a calming rhythm.

"Joe, we really need to talk about this."

"I know," he said with a sigh, flopping down in a comfortable FoamGel chair. "Listen, I know you're not really that into Journalism, but this is really important to me, and I might never get another chance. This whole L5P thing could be big. Really big."

Mary sat down on his lap and wound her arms around his neck. "I know," she said in resignation. Truth be told, she'd made her decision sometime earlier today, seeing how passionate Joe was about the whole matter. "All right," she agreed, somewhat reluctantly, "I will go to L5P with you. It really sounds kind of exciting, and it seems like there is a lot at stake. But you have to promise me that I get to pick our next project."

"It's a deal!" Joe exclaimed, his dark eyes glowing as he leaned forward and kissed her enthusiastically. "You're the best girlfriend a guy could ever have."

"And don't you forget it," she told him with a laugh.

"It is OK if I call Sam now and tell him our decision?" Joe asked, fairly vibrating with excitement.

"Sure," she said with a shrug, getting off his lap and sitting down in the seat beside him.

"Room, call Sam," Joe said.

There was a little wait-time music and finally Sam appeared on the room's huge screen,

"Hi, you guys." Sam said. "I assume you two are all done screwing each other and finally ready to face the music and make some decisions?"

"Yeah," said Joe, while Mary giggled. "We've decided that we're in."

"Excellent," Sam said approvingly. He gave Mary a wink, obviously relieved.

"So who's this guide you know?" Joe asked, ready to get down to business.

"We call him Squiggles because he scrambles his communications," Sam said. "He doesn't want to give his real name just to avoid getting into trouble. He currently runs a shuttle and takes supplies from ISS to L5P and the MoonBase. He also used to take tourist and wanna-be Pilgrims to L5Pilgrim but now that has become a hot potato so he is restricted to government-approved officials and supplies. The government thinks L5P brainwashes people into joining and once somebody joins, their bodies deteriorate so they can never come back. That is the argument against them and it sounds like a good one. He hates it when all you hear is government news and wants better coverage of what is going on, but he doesn't want to lose his supply contract so we gotta be careful. I'll try and reach him now."

There was static and distortion and then an older, curly-haired, rather rough-looking character popped onto the screen. This was obviously Squiggles.

"Yeah, what's up?" Squiggles asked cantankerously.

"We got a couple of reporters who want to interview Dylan Thomas at L5Pilgrim," Sam replied.

"Man, I hate this," Squiggles said. "I mean, I want to do it because I know Amy, and I kind of sympathize with her but the politicians are making it almost impossible for us to let anyone in now. I don't want to lose my contract. I'll tell you what, let's do it like this: you send them up here to do a story on transports so they can ride around with us. I go from International to L5Pilgram to MoonBase and then back to L5Pilgrim and back to International. So I will leave things open at L5Pilgrim so they can just walk away and I will pick them back up a day or so later on my way back. That way I leave ISS with them and return with them. I am gonna play dumb and say I didn't see you get off and stay off. Now we never had this conversation, and we won't have any more conversations, OK? Just do it. "

"Sounds great to me," Joe said, giving Mary a happy look.

"Kinda exciting," Mary admitted. She was finally getting into the whole drama.

"OK – done." Squiggles ran his fingers distractedly through his wild hair. "Sam will make the arrangements for you. Just show up at the SpacePort early tomorrow."

With that, Squiggles disappeared from the screen.

"OK, we gotta do this quick," Sam said. "Can you leave early tomorrow?"

"Yeah," said Joe and Mary simultaneously.

"OK, be at the SpacePort at nine tomorrow morning" said Sam and the communication ended.

"Wow." Mary leaned over and kissed Joe again. "This is exciting. I'm going to get scanned for some clothes now."

Mary walked to the bathroom and undressed. "Room, I am going to the International Space Station tomorrow for a one-week trip."

A soft voice said, *"All right, Mary – please step in to be scanned."*

Mary walked into a large cylinder, put her feet on the markers and reached out with both hands to grab onto a bar. The computer said, *"Scanning now."* It did a complete 360-degree scan of Mary's body.

She remembered that in the old days, people actually used to haul around large boxes called suitcases filled with clothes. There was no need for that now. The measurements taken were sent to any hotel Mary was going to be at and a Replicator there would make her whatever clothes she needed for her visit when she arrived.

When she was done, she grinned. This was going to be so much fun!

Chapter 4

Trip to the Space Port

Early the next morning, Mary and Joe walked groggily to the Main Dome in Joe's house, holding hands and still lost in memories of the amazing night they'd had. After Mary had agreed to go with Joe, they had made love for hours. Both of them felt like this was a major turning point in their relationship. They were going to stay together, no matter what, and this adventure had proved it. Mary had jumped completely onboard with the idea once she'd made her decision, and she could tell how pleased Joe was with her.

He should be, she thought smugly. Not many guys had such great, supportive girlfriends.

Giving her a big grin, he kissed her quickly. "Thanks for doing this."

She nodded. "When are we leaving?"

He looked at the digital display at the wall. "We should head to the SpacePort in the next fifteen minutes or so."

Tired, but smiling, she was thrilled to see her adorable little blonde sister, Daisy, had come over to play with Bobby. "Daisy," Mary cried, holding out her arms. "I didn't know you were coming over to play with Bobby."

Daisy ran over to give her a hug. She was wearing a ridiculous Space Ranger costume.

Alice gave her a harried look from across the room. "Yes, Daisy has been wanting to come over, so I thought today would be good. Bobby was excited by everything he saw at Project Day, but he was really intrigued by the Space Ranger Project."

Mary glanced over at Bobby and laughed. He'd obviously had the Replicator make him a Space Ranger uniform. Of course, the uniform was a little over the top. Bobby had made himself commanding officer with a lot more stars and awards on his uniform than could possibly be awarded.

"I am a Space Ranger!" Bobby cried, running up to Mary and Joe, glad for a new audience. "Look at me. I am a Space Ranger."

"We are going to save the planet from the meteors," Daisy said. "They can destroy us. We have to stop them. We are going to explore Europa. We will save the planet. We are Space Rangers. We have to go to the KiddieDome now." Daisy was dressed as a much lower-ranking officer. She looked a little confused by Bobby's game but she was trying to be a good sport and Mary tousled her blonde hair affectionately.

"Have fun, Daisy," Mary told her little sister. "Joe and I are going on a project, so I won't see you for a while."

Daisy gave a little pout at that, but Bobby grabbed her hand, babbling about Europa and pulled her toward the KiddyDome, and Daisy soon forgot Mary was even there.

Mary watched for a moment as the two children started playing Space Rangers in the KiddieDome, which allowed for a full 360-degree immersion in the game they were playing. Anything they could imagine popped up on the screen, allowing them to explore the Universe any way they wanted to. The computer was also programed to incorporate learning into their play, occasionally weaving in lessons on how to do things and giving reasons for them to need to do things like simple math problems.

'The BubbleVan is here," Joe announced, calling Mary's attention away from the kids. She thanked Alice for her hospitality, then ran outside with Joe, her heart racing as she thought about what they were about to do. It might be dangerous, but she didn't care. She and Joe could handle anything, as long as they stayed together.

One of the great things about BubbleVans was that you could use the time you are traveling to catch up on the news or whatever communications you have neglected. As the car took off, Joe called up some background information on L5Pilgrim that Sam had left him.

Sam's face popped up as Joe played the video voice message Sam had left. "There are a few important characters you need to meet when you get to L5Pilgrim. Amy Worthington is the only contact we have, but people like Jack Noble handle a lot of the science. The most important person is Dylan Thomas, who was elected as the head of L5Pilgrim. He is the only person who can testify and commit L5P to an agreement. Bruno Nightfire is moving quickly to get the directors of ISS to allow him to invade L5P. The reason I feel sad about it is that we don't know the full story. Maybe everyone is brainwashed and for all we know maybe L5Pilgrim should be destroyed. Not all stories have a fairy-tale ending. Anyhow. I will monitor the stream from your SavvyCams and use it as some testimony."

The transmission ended.

Mary frowned a bit. "You know, I really know so little about this whole situation. I wasn't monitoring it at all until you brought it up yesterday, so I'm feeling really unprepared. Can we use this time in the car on the way to the Space Port to learn a little more about ISS and what happened to bring this situation to a head?"

"Of course," Joe replied, giving her a quick grin, obviously glad that she was showing some enthusiasm for the project. "Car, call Welcome Wagon for International Space Station."

"Yeah," said Mary. "I always like to see the images."

The inside of the bubble lit up as though they were in space, an endless void of blackness punctured by the billions of pinpricks of light that made up the Milky Way. Slowly the view rotated and Earth came into view. Then as the camera continued to rotate, ISS came into view and it was absolutely huge.

"*Something in our soul is attracted to space, and nobody can put their finger on it,*" a soft voice began, narrating the welcome for ISS. "*We came from the empty void of space and are called to return to it. In the year 2015, people from Earth first began making regular flights into space. It did not take long for entrepreneurs to see people's desire to go into space, so we began to develop the first SpaceHotels. When it was clear that the hotels were a success, we began the first truly enormous space habitat, which is now the International Space Station.*

"*The International Space Station is composed of two rings,*"

*based on the Stanford Torus. Each ring is hundreds of kilo-
meters wide and the station rotates just enough to give a very
earth-like gravitational pull. Almost everything you have on
Earth can be found here, including rivers, mountains, birds
and wildlife."*

"*There is a traffic delay ahead,*" the car's computer interrupted. "*We left early, so we should still make our flight.*"

"Car, why is there a delay?" Joe asked.

"*We are approaching a major Renovator Project,*" the
computer said. "*Traffic is slowing down to see the Renovators.*"

"Wow," said Joe. "That's right. We are going right past Old
Town, and they are renovating the whole area."

'Oh," Mary exclaimed. "I've never actually seen the Renovators from close up at work before. Can we slow down just
a few minutes and watch them?"

"Of course," Joe said, momentarily distracted from their
own project. Though neither of them had any desire to work
on a Renovator, they both knew that it was supposed to be
quite amazing to actually see how they were able to take huge
chunks of urban decay and transform them into pristine new
suburbs.

"Car, suspend ISS program for a moment and give us a
view of the Renovators," Joe said.

The starscape disappeared, and the BubbleVan's dome
went clear and transparent, giving them a clear 360-degree
view of the world outside. Even though they were still encased
by the bubble, they could easily have been riding around in a
convertible, because the sights and sounds were so vivid. They
had come upon a large traffic jam of BubbleVans, whose oc-

cupants had all done the same thing. Everyone was looking in awe at what was outside.

To the left, an enormous whoosh of sound pierced Mary's ears as a MagLev bullet train zoomed by so fast she wouldn't have even seen it if she hadn't been looking in that direction to start with. As far as the eye could see, this part of the city was a wasteland. She knew that in preparation for the Renovators, they had cleared this part of the city out, but it was hard to believe anyone had ever lived in these buildings. Shattered glass and gaping holes were the norm, with rusted out old cars decaying in front of ramshackle buildings. Mary was glad that with the advent of Renovator technology, the areas that looked like this were getting fewer and fewer. Once the Renovators were done, the people who had lived in this terrible neighborhood would be able to move back in to the home that would literally emerge overnight.

As they crested a hill, they entered what appeared to be a war zone, and Mary flinched a bit at the cacophony of sights and sounds. The deafening noise hurt her ears, but she didn't ask the car to turn it down. She wanted to experience this whole thing.

Thousands of WorkerBots scurried around the desolate landscape, planting charges in the buildings and blowing them up. Helicopter-like bots called ChopperBots set charges on the rooftops, sometimes even firing missiles when the buildings proved stubborn and refused to collapse. Periodically, some of the WorkerBots were crushed by the falling debris, but that was the good thing about bots, you could always make new ones. She couldn't imagine how many lives would be lost or how much time it would take if they tried to do this with actual people doing the work.

"These are the PrepBots," Joe told her. "Their duty is to raze this entire section down to a pile of debris no more than half a story tall."

Mary nodded. She'd heard about it, but found the spectacle absolutely amazing to watch.

The van crept slowly forward over the next hill, and at last the Renovators came into view. They were huge, larger than Mary had imagined, even though she'd known they were big. Dozens of them ground slowly across the piles of debris left by the PrepBots, and each one was enormous, at least two city blocks wide, three city blocks long and five stories tall. Mounted on enormous tank treads, they made indescribable amounts of noise as they inched forward, plumes of smoke belching from their numerous smokestacks.

"The Renovators take the debris in there, you see," Joe said, putting his arms around her and pointing to the end of the Renovator that faced the debris field in front of it. "They basically work like a Replicator, only on a much larger scale."

Mary smiled and nodded. She actually knew quite a bit about the project, but she thought it was cute when he went all manly and tried to explain things to her that he thought were guy things.

"I can't wait until we get to other side of this beast and get to see what comes out the other end," he exclaimed as they inched past it.

Mary gazed up at the huge machine, watching people scurry around on its huge multi-level decks with a lot of excitement. A huge sign on the side of the Renovator said *Caterpillar Renovator RX288*. Below the sign was a radiation label, since the Renovators ran on nuclear power.

Finally they reached the other side of it, and Mary gasped at what she saw. In the wake of the Renovator were miles upon miles of beautiful new homes, office buildings and parks. She was amazed at how each home and building seemed to be a little different, not just cookie cutter squares that all looked the same.

In the wake of the Renovators were the CleanUpBots, which turned the huge depressions left by the Renovator tracks into roads and parks, and generally just cleaned up, ensuring that all the buildings were immediately ready for their new inhabitants.

"That was amazing," Mary breathed, a little awed.

Joe nodded. "I know, right? Almost makes you want to join a Renovator Project."

They looked at each other and burst out laughing. "Ok," he said. "Maybe not."

"Can you imagine? All that noise and chaos every day? They must wear earplugs. Even so, I think it would get pretty boring after you'd seen it all day every day."

"Yeah, my thoughts exactly," Joe agreed. "But I'm still glad we got to see it."

"I know." Mary smiled and pointed a few blocks further on, to where people were pouring back into the neighborhood, obviously thrilled with their new homes. They saw people hugging and laughing, dancing around on their new green lawns. It must be amazing to have come from what was here before just a short time ago and now be moving into a nice, modern home. She especially felt glad for the little children she saw, running around happily, screeching at the sight of swimming pools and playgrounds.

"Well," Mary said, finally turning away from the happy scene. "That was fun. But I guess it's time to get back to business. I still have a lot to learn about ISS."

Joe hugged her and then released her, settling back into his seat. "Car, restart ISS Welcome video."

Chapter 5

Space Flight

Arrivals and departures at the SpacePort were timed so well that when you arrived, you just walked out and your Bubble Van, which knew your arrival time to the minute, was waiting at the curb. A long line of BubbleVans would be waiting, and so people skinned the vans so whoever they were waiting for could find it. So the vans were covered with graphics that said *Daddy George* or *Great-aunt Lucy* or *Happy Anniversary Bob & Sue*, accompanied by pictures and even favorite songs blaring through speakers. As a result, it was a real carnival of flashing lights and videos.

Mary had always loved the excitement, and she peered out with a grin as they approached the departure line. She'd spend the rest of the ride here learning everything she could about ISS and was ready to begin their adventure. She grabbed Joe's hand and fairly skipped into the terminal.

"Can you believe that in just a few moments we're going

to be leaving the Earth's surface?" she exclaimed, beaming up at him, really in the spirit now.

"I can't believe neither of us has been off planet before." He grinned back at her, squeezing her hand as they navigated their way to the gate where their space plane was located. The hallways were lined with high resolution video ads for different space hotels and travel adventure groups for things like space walks, theme parks, and flying in zero gravity. People loved to vacation on ISS because of the perfect weather and the variety of activities that weren't possible on Earth.

SpacePlanes from all the major carriers lined the terminal. As Mary and Joe reached their flight to ISS, they were instantly recognized by transmissions from their SavvyCams and their facial features. They didn't have any baggage, because the Replicator in their hotel room on ISS would make everything they needed.

They were able to immediately board the plane, and they were shown to their own private cubicle for two. The space was surprisingly comfortable and well-equipped with every luxury and high-tech device imaginable to keep people from being bored during their flight.

As soon as the plane took off, Joe contacted Squiggles. Unfortunately, whenever you ran communications through the SpacePlane's servers they had the right to advertise, so the video screen was peppered with ads offering massage, discounts, and a ton of special vacation things to do on ISS. Though the ads were annoying, Squiggles' grouchy face was still visible in the center of the screen.

"Hi, there," he told them, looking a bit nervous. "I hope you guys are up for a little adventure. Let's talk later – not now. Once you arrive at ISS, check into your hotel room and I will meet you there. We then need to go to the cargo transport section of the Space Dock at 15:30 GMT, which is about two hours after you arrive. I am running Cargo Flight 889. We will have enough time to take in a short show I think you will like. I'll see you there."

Squiggles started to sign off and then paused. "Oh, yeah. There is no need for you to talk to anybody else until we meet." With that cryptic statement, the transmission ended.

"He's a little paranoid, isn't he?" Mary observed.

Joe shrugged. "With all the tension between ISS and L5P, I guess he has to be. He doesn't want to be caught in the middle of everything when it all goes bad, which is looking more and more like a possibility. Hopefully, we will be able to make a difference."

Mary leaned forward and kissed him. "I love it that you're so passionate about this."

"Well, you made it all possible, and I love you for that."

Things were starting to heat up between them when the computer announced an incoming call from Joe's mother. They broke apart with a groan and tried to look as though they hadn't been doing what they were doing.

"Hey, Joe, Mary? Are you there? How is it going? Did you make your plane?" Alice asked, finally popping up amid the ads.

"Yes, Mom, we made it. The flight is going pretty good so far."

"That's good." She gave him a worried but loving smile. "I just wanted you to know that even though I hate that you're putting yourself in danger, I am really proud of what you're trying to do."

"Thanks," Joe said, flushing a bit with embarrassment, which Mary found adorable.

"I just want you to stay safe and don't take any unnecessary risks," Alice continued. Her serious words were interrupted by Daisy and Bobby running up to her, dressed in some crazy new costumes.

"What are they playing now?" Mary asked, fighting a laugh.

Alice sighed, obviously having had a rough morning keeping up with the two. "First it was Space Rangers, but Bobby saw something in the PlayDome about the Civil Rights Movement, and now they're dressed up as flower children from the 1960s. Would you like to talk to them? They're very excited to know you're going to the Space Station."

"We'd love to talk to them," Joe said with a smile. Mary loved the way he was so patient with his little brother.

"Bobby, Daisy! Talk to your brother and sister," Alice said, getting the children's attention.

Suddenly Bobby and Daisy were on the screen. They were pretending to be at an Easter egg hunt and dressed for the event complete with baskets and eggs. "We are going to march on Washington next," Bobby proclaimed, obviously a bit annoyed to have to stop his play to have to talk to his brother. "We have to get back to the KiddieDome, Joe. We have to march on Washington."

Mary knew the KiddieDome would provide them with an amazingly real experience, providing background characters and correcting parts of their play that were inaccurate. It was a fun and interactive way to learn. Kids could experience all the great moments in history as though they were actually living them. Mary's favorite lesson had always been the first moon-walk, so she supposed it had been inevitable that eventually she'd end up in space.

"We live in the 1960s," Daisy said. She was all about talk-ing – exactly the opposite of Bobby. "We went on an Easter Egg Hunt. They don't have cell phones here! They have to make cars move. They have funny wheels you have to turn. They get into wrecks and people get hurt. They don't know about computers yet. We need to tell them. We need to march on Washington for equal rights. I am learning poetry. We have to go back to the KiddieDome!"

"That's really sweet," said Mary, just barely following her little sister's rapid-fire recitation of her understanding of the 1960s. "I love it! Can you do a poem for me?"

Daisy held up a purple egg that she must have gotten dur-ing her Easter Egg Hunt and recited:

"The egg is what we all come from,
It gives us life and can be undone,
If this our gift we do forsake,
We lose our soul and can't remake."

"Wow, Daisy, that is really good," said Mary, impressed. "Very deep."

"Fantastic, Daisy!" said Joe. "Bobby, when we get back, I will have to do a poem for you."

"Ok," Bobby agreed impatiently. "We have to go now."

"All right, Bobby. I'll see you when we get back." The

kids scampered off, and Alice's worried face came back on the screen.

"Well, I'll let you go now," Alice said with a sigh. "Just promise me you'll be careful."

Joe grinned. "Of course I will, Mom. What could possibly go wrong?"

Chapter 6

ISS

As Mary and Joe's SpacePlane approached ISS, they eagerly turned to the channel on their monitors that allowed them to watch their own landing. Space buoys were scattered all along the outside of the ISS landing platform so they had the option of watching the landing from several different viewpoints; from the buoys, from inside the ISS docking port, or inside the space plane.

"I never really realized how massive it was," Mary commented in awe.

"The rings are 500 kilometers wide," Joe said softly. "Plenty of space to create an ecosystem."

The two enormous rings were connected to a central shaft where the space planes landed. Eight spokes went from the shaft that had the landing pad to the ring, like spokes on a wheel. Mary knew from her research that the rings were where everyone lived, and the spokes were elevator shafts to transport you from the landing pad to the ring and could be used as a quick way to get from one side to another. The central shaft rotated to give the whole thing centrifugal force. The entire structure truly amazed her, and she was suddenly very glad she'd chosen to come here with Joe.

They watched with amazement at the complicated split-second timing necessary to dock the space plane safely, then disembarked with the rest of the passengers. As they walked off the elevator, there were dozens of BubbleVans waiting, right at the curb like on Earth, and one was skinned with their names. They hopped in and made the short trip to their hotel.

When they arrived at the hotel, the facial recognition software at the entrance scanned their faces from a distance and relayed their reservation information to Joe's SavvyCam, which immediately said, *"Room 689. Please take elevator 6."*

The elevator took them to the correct floor without them having to depress any buttons, and following the instructions they were soon entering their luxurious room. Mary ran around checking everything out, and squeaked in excitement when she saw the huge spa tub in the bathing area.

As she quickly stripped to get in the bath, she heard Squiggles pop up on the screen in the other room, talking to Joe. "Hey, you guys," he said. "Glad to see you made it OK. I'll meet you in the lobby in about twenty minutes."

"Ok," Joe agreed and came to join Mary for a quick bath.

"Hotel, play news," said Mary, as she relaxed against the rim of the tub, and the local news came on.

The subject of transmuting the human body was a huge topic because ISS was so close to L5Pilgrim. As she washed her hair, she listened to an argument about whether or not L5P should be forcibly stopped or whether they had the right to choose their own evolutionary fate.

"What do you think about this issue?" she asked as she got out of the bath, dried off, and strode over to the Replicator for some clothes. "Should they be allowed to do whatever they want?" She rather thought so. After all, why was what they did with their bodies anyone else's business?

Joe shrugged as he got out of the tub and wrapped himself in a fluffy towel while he waited for his clothes as well. "I'm a reporter. It's my job to remain impartial."

"But surely you have an opinion," she pressed.

"I really don't," he argued. "I just really want to find out the truth, fairly presenting both sides of the story and get it out there. It's up to the public to decide what to make of it."

She frowned a little as she dressed, realizing that was what would make him a good reporter but a little frustrated by his answer as well. She really wanted to talk about it with him, but didn't want to influence him if that's how he really felt.

Soon they were freshly bathed and outfitted in great ISS outfits and on their way down to meet Squiggles. He looked even antsier than usual, and quickly made it known that he was in a hurry because the clock was running toward when they had to depart for L5P and he wanted to get in a show first.

"Great to meet you," Squiggles told them as he hustled them out of the hotel. "Sometimes we pass the time around here listening to music and singing. Not everyone can come up with original songs, but if you don't have something original, you can always do a cover."

"What's a cover?" Mary asked as she hurried to keep up with him.

"All you do is go back in history and find a song you like and then you do your version of the song." Squiggles ushered them into a waiting BubbleVan at the curb. "It just so happens that my listening to one of the cover songs Slim Jim did is how I got interested in helping you. His song was worried about how we are robotizing the human body to a point that we just become a machine. I saw the changes Amy and her friends are making at L5Pilgrim, and I wanted their side of the story told, so I contacted Sam."

"Who is Slim Jim?" Joe asked as the BubbleVan pulled away.

"Slim Jim's a real kick. We all get together to have fun and recreate an old cowboy dance hall music and do something they called the two-step. Nice and simple, so anybody can do it. Tonight, he's singing the song that first got me interested in how the human body is changing."

The BubbleVan came to a stop and Squiggles got to his feet. "Anyhow, here it is. Let's kill a few minutes and then we gotta go. I think he is going to play *Ghost Borgs in the Sky,* which is the song I told you about. He dug up an old cowboy song called *Ghost Riders in the Sky*. He likes it because the song paints a picture of where we are headed if things don't change. I like it because it makes you think and ask the question: When does the human body and soul die and just a machine remain?"

They entered the dance hall, which was packed with good-spirited people. Everyone was talking about each other's costumes and their boots, which you never normally see. The hall was like a standard dome except with a stage up front where Slim Jim and the boys were tuning up. Mary watched with excitement as they got ready. She hardly ever got to listen to live music back home.

The lights went down, and everyone clapped and lined up to dance.

The dome suddenly went totally dark and then the dome screen displayed a lonely hilltop on Earth. The atmosphere was eerie, like one of those electrifying moments just before a major storm. Huge dark clouds moved swiftly over the hills and the dome recreated the breeze. Then bolts of lightning flashed as the warm summer wind blew around the dance hall.

Then Slim Jim said, "This is based on a popular cowboy song called *Ghost Riders in the Sky* and we call it *Ghost Borgs in the Sky*". He laughed and said, "Will this be our fate?"

Then Slim Jim's band began to play with deep base guitars that matched his deep voice as the thunder and lighting grew louder.

An old cowboy went riding out one dark and windy day

Upon a ridge he rested as he went along his way

When all at once a mighty herd of red eyed Borgs he saw

Plowing through the ragged sky, unable to withdraw

Their circuits were misfiring and their legs were made of steel

Their robot face was black and blue and their hot breath he could feel

A bolt of fear went through him as they thundered through the sky

For he saw our fate A-coming hard and he heard their mournful cry

Yippie yi ohhhhh

Yippie yi yaaaay

Ghost Borgs in the sky

*Their faces gaunt, their eyes were blurred, their shirts all
soaked with sweat*

*They're running hard to find their souls, but they ain't found
'em yet*

'Cause they've got to ride forever on that range up in the sky

In robot bodies made of bolts and listen to their cry

As the Borgs all stomped on by him he heard one call his name

If you want to save your soul from Hell a-riding on our range

Then cowboy change your ways today or with us you will ride

Trying to catch a soul you lost, across these endless skies

Yippie yi ohhhhh

Yippie yi yaaaay

Ghost Borgs in the sky

Ghost Borgs in the sky

Ghost Borgs in the sky

Everybody in the hall seemed to be having a stomping good time, especially when it came to the chorus, where they all chimed in. The two-step added something to the song with hundreds of pounding feet like a marching army of robots. As soon as it was over, everyone was clapping and Squiggles grabbed both Joe and Mary to let them know that they had to go.

Mary felt exhilarated as they rushed out of the dance hall. She had never experienced anything like that. "Thank you for taking us," she told Squiggles. "I really enjoyed it."

Squiggles gave her a quick grin as he ushered them back into the BubbleVan. "I thought you might like it."

As they headed to the cargo ship, Mary and Joe asked Squiggles to leave the bubble clear so they could look out at ISS.

"Wow," said Joe. "I look left to right and I can't tell I am not on Earth, because you can't see the edges of the tube."

"Yeah," said Squiggles. "But if you look carefully up in the sky, you can kind of sense that there is a ceiling. Water does evaporate and it goes up and condenses when it reaches the top of the tube, which is way the hell up there. ISS was an immense project and never could have been done a long time ago, but once we developed the advanced WorkerBots, we had the manpower to do almost anything – we just make as many bots as we need. You can have a whole army of them pretty quick. Even now, we have a zillion WorkerBots constantly going over the surface to maintain it. As far as the final product is concerned, the sunlight is almost Earthlike but a little is lost coming through the tube. We have allowed mountains to be created so we have climate changes. It is still a work in progress, but it is very pleasant. No tornadoes or hurricanes."

"What else do you guys do with all your free time?" Mary asked curiously.

"We do most of the same things you do on Earth," Squiggles replied. "When you have most of your material needs taken care of, what do you do? Well, you do what the great apes do after they have eaten – you sit around and stroke each other. We have massage, beaches, sports, plays, and debates. There are a million things you can do. A big one is exploring space. The Mars Conversion Project is well underway."

They got to the cargo terminal, which looked just like a

cargo terminal on Earth. WorkerBots scurried around every-where, moving pallets of materials from one place to another. There were no other humans around and there so many bots that a time or two Mary and Joe got scolded for being in the wrong place at the wrong time and making the bot come to a stop. A WorkerBot would never run a human over, but they sure let you know when you got in their way.

The cargo ship was actually a giant box. There was no need for aerodynamic design, so it was just a long box that looked like a giant railcar with a lot of sensors on it. The entrance for people was at the midsection and as soon as you got inside the ship you were in the main bridge, which was just a large standard dome room but with lots of extra controls. As soon as they got on board the ship, the doors closed.

"You gotta strap down," Squiggles said. "And I have some housekeeping stuff to do."

The ship took off and floated out of the ISS. Cameras cov-ered the area above the ship, below the ship, both sides of the ship and the front and back of the ship and the screens on the bridge displayed all the different camera angles. Mary watched Squiggles maneuver the huge box with great interest. He could switch to whatever camera interested him and the computer gave verbal warnings if there were any hazards or debris in the area he needed to avoid.

"It looks like a bot could run this ship," Joe commented. "It's all computerized, isn't it?"

Squiggles gave Joe a dirty look. "Bots are good for a lot of things," he said shortly. "But sometimes you need a hu-man, just in case anything goes wrong. If we have bots and computers doing everything, then you run into problems they can't handle, like decisions on political matters like those on

L5P. Not a good thing, if you ask me, to do away with humans completely."

"*L5Pilgrim in range*," said the onboard computer.

The dome lit up with a visual of L5P, which was just like the ISS except it had just one doughnut ring and the whole station was hardly turning at all.

Squiggles made a window on the dome screen for communication with Amy at the L5Pilgrim Portal.

"Ship, scramble communication," Squiggles commanded.

The screen immediately turned into squiggly lines like some sort of test pattern.

"Ship, call Amy at L5P."

A cacophony of dialing and ringing went on, and then finally a female voice came on the line, laughing.

"Oh gosh," said the voice, while other females in the background laughed hysterically. "Who could it possibly be? It's a real mystery." The voice suddenly got serious. "Larry, will you please stop it with the scrambler? It's no wonder everybody calls you Squiggles."

Larry was obviously embarrassed. "Oh, all right." He clicked a few buttons on the screen. "I just wanted to scramble stuff so they can't come back and hassle me. Don't you know that scrambled stuff stays off the log?"

Just then the screen cleared up and Amy floated in mid air in front of the camera with a big smile on her face. A few of her friends floated behind her.

"Life's too short, Larry," Amy smiled. "You can't be worried about all that stuff. If they get pissed off, just tell them it's my fault." Amy threw her hands up in the air and did a backflip in midair. "I love to take the blame!" she said as she appeared back on screen with both arms stretched out.

Mary was amused by Amy's infectious good humor. So far, every time she'd seen anyone from L5P they'd been like this.

"Hey!" Amy said, getting back to business. "Did you bring me those big Replicators and the FixItBots we wanted?"

"Yeah," Larry drug out his words reluctantly, because now he knew he was on the record. "I guess so… they are on the log."

"Who's that behind you?" Amy asked. "I haven't seen them before. This better not be a political thing."

"No," Larry muttered, still obviously uneasy to be talking about any of this without his scrambler. "These are the friends of mine that I told you about."

Everyone at L5P laughed. "Oh yeah," Amy replied, mocking Larry's tone. "These are the *special friends* of yours! Hi, friends! A friend of Larry's is a friend of mine!"

"Amy, can I just drive this ship in and dock?" Larry asked.

"No," Amy told him. "Sorry, no can do. It would take too much time for me to take the screen down and there may be other ships in the area, so let's just let the bots do their normal thing."

"Well…..OK," Larry agreed even more reluctantly. "You will take care of things like we discussed, right?"

Amy held her finger up to her lips. "Ssshhh."

All the other women chimed in with their own rendition of "Sssshhh" as though they were young girls at a slumber party. Mary frowned, a little confused by the way they were acting.

"Mum's the word," giggled Amy and the screen went black except for a big L5P logo in the middle of it.

"So your real name is Larry," said Mary

"Oh all right," Larry snapped, "but Sam should have told you about what we are doing so I don't have to repeat it. Now, I did not see you get off the ship at L5P, there is nothing on the log about it, and I will pick you back up in a day or so on my return trip, which goes from Lunar1 to L5P to ISS, OK?"

"OK," Mary and Joe said simultaneously.

"What do we do once we get off the ship?" asked Mary

"The cargo ship will anchor with magnets because there is almost no gravity on L5P and the bots use air jets to offload the cargo. You will be in almost zero G and there is a huge hole in the wall at the end of the bay. Just kind of jump off the end of the ship and propel yourself toward the hole and Amy will find you. After that, good luck to you. I can't be responsible for what happens."

"OK," said Joe, sounding a little worried.

"Now we gotta put up with this stupid game." Larry sighed. "They don't want tourists and really don't want politicians so they go through a big spiel to try and get rid of visitors."

An alert sounded on the ship's audio. *"Incoming alert message...passage is not safe...turn back immediately!"*

The ship rocked a little bit like something hit it. *"ALERT! ALERT! Passage not authorized! Passage not safe! Your ship will be destroyed. Return immediately!"*

Mary clung to her seat, suddenly nervous, realizing that they were actually in danger, but Larry just rolled his eyes as if to say this was boring. After a few more even more serious warnings, the ship was jolted hard and rocked back and forth. Larry just smiled and waved his hand in the air, letting them know he was not concerned and this would all pass soon. The ship continued to rock.

Mary realized the ship was not just pitching back and forth erratically but doing some sort of dance that Larry seemed to enjoy. She tried to relax, but found that to be rather difficult. She did not enjoy a dancing ship.

Suddenly a song came blasting over the speakers in sync with the ship's movement, a very up-tempo sound of a flute, a violin, and a piccolo and also a few deep pounding drums. Together they made a fantastic background for the deep-voiced song. Mary had the strange sensation that she on the deck of a ship filled with drunken, singing sailors.

Larry began to sing along.

Fifteen men on a dead man's chest
Yo ho ho and a bottle of rum
Space and the gods has called for the rest
Yo ho ho and a bottle of rum.

The first was fixed by the freedom they found
The rest they came so they can't be bound
and they want more people of their kind to surround

Now you can't stop things with muscle and clout
'cause freedom and space are expanding on out
And no man's story can tell what it's all about

Ohhh

Fifteen men on a dead man's chest
Yo ho ho and a bottle of rum
Space and the gods has called for the rest
Yo ho ho and a bottle of rum.

The government knows what it's it all about
They can't let live so they glower and they pout
They need to control so they argue and they shout

Now you can't stop freedom and stick it in a hole
You can't dress it up to make it fit your favorite role
You gotta let the people just expand their soul

Ohhh

Fifteen men on a dead man's chest
Yo ho ho and a bottle of rum
Space and the gods has called for the rest
Yo ho ho and a bottle of rum.

With that intro, everything went absolutely dead quiet and the ship slowly drifted into the L5Pilgrim docking bay. Mary exchanged a half-amused, half-terrified look with Joe. What the hell had they gotten themselves into?

Chapter 7

L5Pilgrim

The transporter drifted into L5Pilgram's huge, well-lit landing bay and locked down using magnets. "Remember," Larry warned them. "We're at almost zero G here, so when you get off, you're going to float a little. You'll settle to the ground eventually, but not for a while."

"What happens after we jump off the back of the ship?" Joe asked.

"Beats the hell out of me," Larry said with a shrug. "My only job was to get you here. See you in a day or so."

Larry stayed with the ship, where the WorkerBots were busy unloading cargo and moving themselves around with air jets. A bunch of ChopperBots flew around like vacuum cleaners, sucking up all the trash and free floating debris.

Joe and Mary exited the ship, holding on to the handles outside of it so they did not float away.

"Joe," said Mary. "Maybe we shouldn't have done this. We can go back, you know."

"I gotta do this, Mary," Joe replied. "I don't think they mean us harm. They could have just told us we are not welcome. Look, there is the big hole in the wall over there."

A really bright light came from a huge round hole in the wall. "I guess holes in the wall make more sense when you're floating around," Mary said with a bit of a laugh. "It would be difficult for us to get to the ground to open a door."

"Let's push off the back of the cargo ship and aim toward the opening," said Joe.

"Hold my hand," said Mary. "I don't think we are going to make it all the way there."

They held hands, counted to three and pushed off as hard as they could toward the big opening.

As they flew through the air, they realized they didn't really have enough of a push to get them to the opening. "We're not going to make it," Mary said in frustration. How were they ever supposed to get anywhere if they just floated aimlessly without any way to propel themselves?

As though in answer, a WorkerBot blasted off the ground and floated up right under them, skinned with a flashing message *Grab Me*. Each of them grabbed one of the giant handles on the WorkerBot and the little Bot propelled them toward the opening. As they exited the docking bay, Mary blinked her eyes in amazement.

Everything was bathed in sunlight and beautiful fields of grass and small mountains stretched before them. The surface of a lake in the distance shimmered like a piece of glass, and there was a warm breeze here, unlike ISS where it had been completely calm.

"It's beautiful here," Mary breathed. "Like a fantasyland."

Before Joe could answer, Amy suddenly dove down from the sky above them, flipped over a few times for fun, and then drifted right in front of them. Behind her was a small flock of her friends, who were carrying some strange small objects, and closing in fast.

Amy wore a white jumpsuit, and jutting from the rear were brightly colored artificial feathers. Attached to her arms and the sides of her body was some kind of material, so that when she stretched out her arms she could glide through the air like a bird.

"Hi, you guys! I'm glad you didn't get scared and go home," Amy said with a big smile.

Amy was just as cheerful and full of life as she looked in all her video appearances. In fact, she was even more animated in person.

"Oh, we wouldn't have missed it," Joe assured Amy, taking everything in with bright eyes. "I've been really hoping I could get up here and talk to you."

"There will be time for that later," Amy said. "The first thing we have to do is get you two into AstroSuits. You are going to be useless around here until we get that done. The WorkerBot will take you to Jack and he will suit you up."

"That sounds good," Mary said cautiously. An AstroSuit was obviously what Amy was wearing, but she wondered who Jack was.

Amy could not take it any longer and turned to her friends, who had been hovering silently behind her, waiting patiently for her to finish talking. They all eyed Mary and Joe with interest. "OK, I give up!" she said, throwing her hands up. "What are those things?"

Everybody started laughing.

"Larry told us he was going to take your friends to a place at ISS where they had strange music instruments from way back in the 1970s and everyone dressed up like cowboys and they had a real blast. So we went and looked up some of the instruments and had the replicator make them," one girl exclaimed enthusiastically, holding up what looked like a banjo.

"Yeah," said another woman. "Now we want to form a band and write a song!"

"Sounds like fun to me," said Amy. "But I don't think any of us can write a song and the music has to fit the instruments."

A little silence fell, because no one seemed to have thought of that.

"Why don't you just do a cover?" Mary asked, remembering what Larry had told her when they'd gone to the dance hall.

They all just stared at her, obviously unfamiliar with the term, but no one wanting to be the first to admit it. Mary grinned a little, waiting for the inevitable question.

"What's a cover?" someone finally asked.

"All you do," Mary said. "Is go back in the history and find a song. Then you change it a little and sing your version of the song. All the work is already done for you."

"Yeah!" a few of them said together.

"That sounds great," said Amy. "Let's do it." She turned to Joe and Mary and gave them a grin. "Ok, this nice WorkerBot is going to take you to Jack Noble, and he will get you both into an AstroSuit. Then you can explore L5P a bit, and get a feel for how we do things here."

"I'm just curious," said Mary. "Where does the name L5Pilgram come from?'

"Well," said Amy. "Technically, the L is a mathematical

term and stands for a Lagrange Point or Lagrange Area. Just suffice it to say that it is an area of stable gravitational equilibrium located along the path of the moon's orbit, 60 degrees ahead or behind the moon. It has the characteristic that an object placed in orbit in the L5 area will remain there indefinitely without having to expend fuel to keep its position. Once we created our community here, the people voted to live in almost zero gravity. Large groups of people have come here for just that reason so they started calling us the L5Pilgrim community or L5P because we are like pilgrims in a new world."

"We'd really like to talk to Dylan Thomas," Joe told Amy before she could fly away, anxious to complete his mission.

A slight murmur went through the flock, and Amy smiled at them. "Dylan doesn't see just anybody," she answered. "We don't even know you yet. You're lucky we let you come here at all. We don't let very many people in, you know. But Larry vouched for you, so here you are."

Joe cleared his throat, obviously realizing he'd overstepped himself. "I'm not trying to be pushy. I just really want to understand you guys and what you're trying to do here."

It seemed as though all they were interested in was flying around and having fun, Mary thought, staring at the girls speculatively. They didn't seem at all worried about what ISS was planning, and she wondered if any of them were even aware that their entire way of life hung in the balance. Joe might be the only thing that could keep Bruno Nightfire from destroying this place. She was suddenly very proud of her boyfriend.

Amy eyed Joe for a long moment as though trying to read his mind and decide whether or not he was really here to try to help them. Then she shrugged and laughed again. "Later we'll talk," she reiterated. "For now, go get an AstroSuit so you don't float away."

With a laugh, she turned back to her flock, and they all darted away.

Joe turned to Mary with a sigh. "She doesn't seem to be taking this very seriously."

Mary laughed. "I think something in the air up here keeps people from being too serious. They all seem so happy, don't they?"

The WorkerBot began zooming over the landscape, and they held on tightly, aware that they'd be in trouble if they let go.

Joe nodded. "They certainly don't seem like a danger to anybody, that's for sure."

As Mary and Joe glided through the air, they were treated to a view of how incredibly different life was here. Homes were perched high on hillsides, but there were no roads going to them. Large buildings sprouted in the middle of nowhere. Mary supposed that made sense, because the people of L5P apparently just flew everywhere they wanted to go, so there was no need for roads.

The WorkerBot flew toward a small mountain. As they crested the tree-covered peak, a small city stretched before them. An incredible view of lakes and a pristine green river valley stretched before them, and the buildings were light and airy, with huge decks facing the incredible view, which made Mary think they must all spend a lot of time outside. The decks appeared to serve two purposes, she realized as she watched people come and go from them. In addition to viewing, they also seemed to be like small landing strips, so people could fly in large items or whole groups of people.

The WorkerBot finally began to slow, losing altitude above one house in particular, lowering them for a perfect landing on top of the deck. They'd apparently arrived at Jack's house.

Chapter 8

Suzie and the Flock

Jack's place was more like a huge artist's studio than a house. As Mary and Joe were whisked inside by their host, she had a quick impression of a ton of work benches, all kinds of electronic equipment, and oven-like machines.

"Welcome to L5P," said Jack, a tall, smiling man with dark hair. "I know you're gonna love it here! We have sunlight for most of the 24-hour day with maybe five hours of darkness so the plants don't go crazy."

"Hello," Mary said, grinning at his energy. Everyone she'd met here so far seemed happy and energetic.

"I took your size information from the ISS hotel replicator," Jack said, as he handed them their suits. "So the suits should fit. I made slits on top of the shoulders so your Savvy-Cam can poke through. Go ahead and try them on and then I will show you the other tools you need to get around."

Mary and Joe took the bundles of fabric and gave each

other a confused look as they shook them out and saw how much fabric they consisted of. "How do you get in this thing?" Mary asked.

Jack laughed and showed her where to put her arms and legs. "When you stretch out your arms, you will see that the fabric under your arms is also attached to your side. That gives you wings when you stretch your arms out, just like a bird," said Jack. "You also have a tail to help you fly. When you open your arms to make a wing, the tail material will open up and stiffen just like with many birds. Your shoes are also slightly magnetized so when you land on metal, like the floor of all the decks and homes, you will be lightly anchored but it is not much of a force – flapping your wings or jumping will dislodge you right away You will learn how to use everything fairly quickly."

"That's awesome," Joe said, giving his arms an experimental flap.

"Oh yeah," Jack said. "If you are new to L5P and feel uncomfortable, most buildings do have a room or two that is a centrifuge so you could go into the room, turn on the centrifuge and then it is like on Earth where you can sit around in chairs, etc. but the people who have been here for a long time hardly ever do that. In fact, if you have been here a long time you don't want to use the centrifuge at all because it is too much of a strain on your system. Everyone just floats and flies around."

"How do you stay afloat?" asked Joe

"Easy," said Jack. "You have little air turbines around your suit and you have the ability to direct the air whichever way you want. You can verbally say what you want to do by just talking to your SavvyCam or you can actually press some buttons to blast yourself around this way or that. A common command is to say 'AstroSuit, still,' and air jets will blast to keep you motionless in one position in the sky."

Mary looked down at her suit, locating the buttons he indicated.

"But," Jack went on, "you usually don't want to do that because you can also move yourself up in the air by flapping your wings. We are really just like birds here but with less energy expended."

"How do you guys sleep?" asked Joe

"Simple," said Jack. "We just create a box that is sort of like a four-sided cargo net. You just float in one end and close the door. Then you float around inside, bouncing off the walls during the night. It's really very comfortable."

Mary frowned a bit at this, thinking that it didn't sound very comfortable to bounce around all night, but maybe it was better than it sounded.

"Yeah! You guys are looking pretty good," Jack exclaimed once they'd finally gotten all the way suited up. "Let's open the door and give it a work out. Why don't you just jump off the deck?"

Things almost never work right the first time and flying was no exception. Joe and Mary were really excited and walked to the edge of the patio. As they jumped off the patio deck, both of them wanted to hot rod it around in their new AstroSuits.

Joe immediately hit his blaster to go hard right and Mary immediately hit her blaster to go hard left. They slammed into each other and then broke apart, laughing.

"Hey! You kids have got to be a little careful at first," Jack yelled at them from his deck. "We have accidents here all the time." He looked off in the distance and said, "Oh, man. Now I gotta do a report."

Speeding toward them were two people with a large box-like structure between them. Behind them were a flock of about ten people, all giggling and laughing as they sailed around each other. The high positive spirits seemed to be infectious here. Finally everybody was close enough so Joe and Mary could see a big red cross on the box.

Jack floated out a few feet to greet them. "Sorry, guys. I am just suiting some newbies up for the first time and they are all thumbs."

The two medics laughed, and one of them peered at Mary. "You guys sure you are all right? Those suits you are wearing have a crash alarm in them in case you bang real hard into a wall or mountain. We have that stuff happen from time to time."

"I guess the big box is an ambulance?" Joe asked.

"You got it." said one medic.

"Who are all the people following you?" Mary asked, looking out at the small crowd a bit uncomfortably.

"Oh, they are just ambulance chasers." said the other medic with a smile.

At this point, the people chimed in with excitement and laughter. "What's your name? Where do you come from? How long are you going to be here? Do you want to take a tour?"

One member of the flock said, "Yeah! Let's take them on a tour!"

"Yeah," several of the others said in unison.

Joe and Mary smiled and looked over to Jack for approval.

Mary could tell Joe was hoping he'd get some good info for his story, but she was kind of just along for the ride, so she was happy to see anything.

"This is Joe and Mary," Jack replied. "OK, you can take them around but bring them back when you are done because I have to take them back to Amy after they get used to the AstroSuits."

The ambulance guys took off and two people grabbed Joe and two grabbed Mary. The whole flock started to fly off toward a lake in the distance.

As they were flying through the air, the two people holding Mary let go and Mary glided through the air. Then one woman flipped upside down and zoomed up under Mary so she was now facing Mary but under her.

"Hi, there!" she said with a smile. "My name is Suzie. Are you ready for some fun?"

"Yeah," said Mary. "What should I do?"

"Hold your hands out like this," Suzie said. She stretched her arms straight out, exposing her wings and also automatically bringing out her tail feathers.

Mary opened her arms, but she was kind of awkward and gangly – she was not exactly clear where everything should go and her feet were all over the place.

"You have got to put your feet together," said Suzie as she went down to Mary's legs and pushed them together.

Suzie popped back up in front of Mary. "Just kind of stiffen your body a little and the legs will go straight and position themselves right under your tail and everything will be in line."

Mary stiffened up and tried to strike a pose with her arms outstretched.

"Yeah," said Suzie. "You got it! Now I am going to get a little ahead of you, and I will be just below you. So all you have to do is copy whatever I do. OK?"

"OK," said Mary

Susie got just under and ahead of Mary. She flapped her wings five times and then just stretched her arms out and glided. Mary copied every movement and found herself gliding too.

"Damn, this is exhilarating!" Mary cried. She had never experienced anything like it. She was actually flying!

"Yeah," giggled Suzie. "It is amazing how much power you get from flapping your wings because there is almost no gravity. They adjusted the centrifugal force so it is perfect for flying. Let's go see about your boyfriend."

Suzie made a right turn, and Mary followed her. Joe was getting the same type of instructions from another member of the flock.

Suzie pulled up in front of Mary, pulled her wings in, and turned 180 degrees so she was facing Mary.

"Now straighten up like this," said Suzie. She was straight up and down with her feet to the ground. Mary was a little awkward but managed to do the same thing.

"Now say 'Suit, still'," said Suzie.

"Suit, still," Mary commanded, and she could hear the little air jets adjusting her position.

"You notice how you are not drifting down at all?" said Suzie. "The gear in your suit adjusts your position with little blasts of air to keep you pretty much stationary. So we could sit here and talk all day and not move an inch."

"That's cool," Mary said enthusiastically.

"Copy my words," said Suzie "Suit, Joe arm's distance."

Mary said the same thing. The AstroSuits drifted them over to Joe.

"Hi, Joe," said Suzie. "So I was just telling Mary the suit commands. You can give your suit a name if you want to and that will become the operative word. The AstroSuits recognize your voice, so they don't get you mixed up with someone else. If you ever get a bad command, just say 'Suit stop' and it stops whatever it was doing."

"I hear you have all kinds of landscape designs for flying around," said Joe.

"Yeah," several people said with excitement.

"Let's do jungle tunnels," said someone.

"OK," said Suzie "But Joe and Mary, because you are new at this, why don't you say 'Suit, track Suzie'. Then you just flap along right behind me and if you stray off course the AstroSuit will adjust things and keep you right in line with me."

"OK," said Mary. "Suit, track Suzie."

"Yoo-hoo," said someone "Let's go!"

The whole flock, including Joe and Mary, took off.

Everyone flapped toward a mountain range. The mountains here were almost totally covered with greenery. Some mountains were extremely steep, some were a gradual climb, and some were just rolling hills.

Everyone was headed toward a very steep mountain and as

they got close Mary could see that a quarter of the way down the mountain was a huge circular hole that went right through the mountain and there was light from the other side. Flowers of every color were arrayed around the hole. As they zoomed through the hole, a dozen more tunnels came into view on the other side.

Flying through the tunnels was absolutely exhilarating. The weather changed from warm to cold and the beauty of all the flowers and plants was indescribable. The sights and scents were so utterly foreign Mary didn't even know what to compare them to. Parts of the tunnels were like echo chambers and everyone was making animal noises as they flew through them. The collective voices echoed oddly. Mary couldn't remember the last time she'd had so much fun.

Mary decided it was a good thing that Suzie had told them to track her or they probably would never have been able to keep up and would have been bouncing into walls all over the place. As it was, they tracked her easily, so they really didn't have to worry too much about the technique of flying, though as they kept on, Mary thought she was starting to get it.

As they came out of the fifth tunnel, the people up front were slowing down. Up in the sky ahead of them a lot of other people were flying in one direction toward the top of a mountain.

"It's SkyBall," said Suzie. "Let's go take a look."

"What's SkyBall?" Joe asked.

"You'll see," Suzie replied with a laugh.

As they got closer and closer to the top of the mountain, the density of people increased. Everyone slowed down so they wouldn't hit each other.

As they flew over the top of the mountain, Mary saw a huge stadium, just like a large football field and what looked like bleachers. The bleachers were black metal strips and they were fairly wide — about as wide as the length of five cars.

"The bleachers are just magnetic strips," said Suzie. "Your shoes are magnetized so you can just land on them. Since you are almost weightless, you can stand on them like a bird sits on a wire except you will not feel uncomfortable because there is no gravity pulling you down. You can see that the distance between the rows of the bleachers is far enough apart that nobody is blocking anybody's view."

As they landed on the bleachers, Mary and Joe looked out at the unusual stadium. There was an actual football field down on the ground and ten large rings of different colors connected side by side and suspended out in front of you and not on the field. The rings acted just like lanes at a track and field event. Then there was another set of the same rings 100 meters away and then another set and another set — going all the way around the area covered by the football field below.

"Oh yeah," said Suzie, "I don't know if you have figured it out yet or not but this is as much of a social event as it is a sporting event. People land on the bleachers and walk around and talk to each other while watching the game. It is kind of a combination of socializing and watching the game. Just like on Earth, but you can move around more here. People also can jump from bleacher to bleacher as the spirit moves them."

Joe and Mary looked down at the stadium. There was a nice manicured grassy field all painted up like any football field but the goal posts extended from the field all the way up to the highest bleacher in the stadium.

"You are probably wondering why they have the rings

around the stadium like a track event," said Suzie. "They are going to play SkyBall, but before the game starts they have a short race to decide who gets to defend which goal. Look up in the sky and you will see ten flyers. Five are the red team and five are the blue team. When the horn sounds, they all zoom down and go through all the hoops. If you miss a hoop, you have to go back and go through it. They all race around the stadium once and the first team to get three of their players over the finish line wins and their team gets to pick which goal to defend."

"What's SkyBall?" asked Joe again.

"Sorry, I forgot to explain that," laughed Suzie. "It's basically soccer in 3D. Imagine that the field of play is the football field you see on the ground extended up in the air to the highest bleacher in the stadium. That makes a giant box. Since there is almost no gravity, you can zoom around anywhere in the box. As you can imagine, there are a lot of chest balls and headers in this game."

What happens when the ball goes out of bounds?" asked Joe.

"The ball has sensors in it," said Suzie. "If it hits the imaginary boundary of the box then air jets inside the ball fire off and the ball bounces off the imaginary wall. They start the game by kicking off in the middle of the box. There is also another game called EarthBall just over the hill in the stadium next to us. Let's watch a little of SkyBall and then go see some EarthBall."

Joe and Mary noted that everyone was walking around and talking about their favorite player. Lots of team colors and people who skinned their AstroSuits with player's jersey numbers and even pictures of their favorite player. Everybody moved to the edge of the bleacher. Then the horn sounded for the start of the race.

The ten players were flapping their wings like crazy and dive bombing down to the rings. Everyone was hollering for their favorite player as they zoomed around the rings. There was a little jostling here and there and some players bounced off the ring and had to backtrack to go through the ring they missed. Of course everyone screamed about how their player clearly got cheated and there were instant replays on the giant screen at the ends of the field, which never really seemed to end the arguments.

Joe and Mary wandered over to a group of the red shirts who were hot and bothered. They kind of glanced at Mary and were not sure if she was friend or foe.

"Did you see that!" said Mary, knowing what they wanted to hear. "The red shirt guy was clearly fouled! The blue shirt guy clearly pushed him into the rim of the ring."

Job done.

Everyone enthusiastically agreed and half the people shook Mary's hand. That's all you really had to do to become an accepted member of the red tribe and the method had worked since the dawn of civilization. From then on, it was all good feelings and lots of detailed analysis on how it was both elbow and leg that were in contact.

After a short while, Mary stepped over to Joe and kissed him on the cheek and whispered in his ear, "Booorrrring!" Joe and Mary both hated sports and had never really been into any sport. The appeal of sports on L5P had quickly worn off.

Joe and Mary looked around and there were some people standing back from the edge that were just talking about whatever was newsy today. Mary wandered over.

It was time for the old slow walk technique to break the ice. She pretended she was slowly walking past the group of people going somewhere so she couldn't help but "accidentally" overhear the conversation. Then if she liked the conversation she could act concerned and stop and add her feelings.

"I don't see how the ISS can do it!" said jersey number three. "They have no right, and I don't care what the politicians say. This is not their land."

"Yeah," said jersey number fourteen, "but that does not stop them. They don't give a damn and anything that threatens the smooth running of the ISS is toast."

"Hi. I'm Mary and I couldn't help overhearing what you were saying. I guess you are talking about ISS shutting down L5P?" said Mary as Joe wandered over. "Why do you think they want to do it? Something about evolution?"

"Yeah," said number three. "They like to pretend we are a cult or something. Poor innocent minds who have been brainwashed by Dylan Thomas."

"Yeah," added number six. "And they feel they have to do an intervention and save us from ourselves. We are obviously not intelligent enough to know how we want to live our lives because we are not living like them. Anybody who is not like them is mentally deranged. Go figure that one."

"I think it is the news," said number eight. "You get the most attention for your newscast if you turn someone into a villain and paint them evil. Explaining both sides of an issue is dull and boring. So it does not pay to have good journalism because you simply do not get many eyes and ears so you do not make much money."

"But isn't there some reasoning behind their concerns?" said Mary. "I mean none of you can go back to Earth because your bone structure has changed so drastically."

"Is that a promise?" said three with a smile.

"Oh! What will I ever do?" said four and everyone laughed.

"Mary, it's the other way around," said eight. "They can never come live with us and enjoy the great life we have because they are so enslaved to living on the rock called Earth. Therefore we can say that they should be punished because they are not progressive — we are the future."

"They say people have died by going completely zero G and their bodies could not handle the transition," said Mary

"Absolutely true," said eight, "but you are talking about the outer fringe. The people who are pushing the envelope and choosing to have no human body structure at all. The way they see it, the WorkerBots and FixItBots can supply everything they need. They only have to be able to communicate with the bots to ask for whatever they need. Some people have died in the evolutionary change to absolute zero G and some live. It is their god given right as intelligent life forms to do whatever they wish and who are we to force our life on them?"

"But what's going to happen?" said Mary. "Where will all this eventually go?"

"God only knows," said eight with a smile, "but I feel that it is natural evolution taking place and not something forced on us. Just let it be and don't play God. Let everyone evolve the way they want to evolve. You don't have to follow them if you don't want to, and who is to say your life is better than theirs?"

"Hey! There you are! I found you," said Suzie. "Let's go

see the EarthBall game. It is just ready to get started now."

The soccer game was in full force now and it looked exciting to watch football played out in a 3D area but Joe and Mary really had no interest. They would have much rather have stayed and kept talking to this group, but they felt they had to stay with Suzie. Otherwise, how would they ever find their way back to Jack's? So Joe, Mary and the flock took off for the next stadium.

It was pretty dense with people in the air because there were two stadiums with games. All the people were smiling and having the time of their life, flying through the air. Mary got tons of friendly greetings from complete strangers.

As they landed on the bleachers for the EarthBall game, they saw that this stadium had pretty much the same setup as the soccer game. The only difference was the goal posts were extremely wide. Up in the air above the stadium was a very large ball covered with an image of the planet Earth.

"OK," said Suzie. "This game is a little different. You see the red team and the blue team. There are twenty-five people on each side and they are standing at their goal post. Now the referee will start the game by pushing the ball down in the middle of the field. The object is for each team to push the ball into the goal post of the opposing team. You can do anything you want to make that happen but you cannot hold another player. Anything else goes."

"Sounds pretty straightforward," said Joe

"Yeah," said Suzie, "but there is a lot to it. Your first thought is to have all your players hit the ball in the center and push it to the goalpost but that is not going to work. Suppose, for example, that the blue team did that and the red team had their players hit the ball in the upper area. The ball would bounce down and probably bounce off the ground and up toward the goal the red team wants to get to. Also it would be foolish not to keep some players in the backfield to defend the goal. Also consider that you can block other players – you just can't hold them. So you can send players around the ball to block other players. It gets to be a real chess game."

The starting buzzer went off and the ball was dropped into the field of play. Everyone in the stands went wild with excitement. Both teams attacked the ball with players spread out all over their side of the ball. A few players were held in the backfield like goalies. It was then a pushing contest except some players from each team snuck around the ball to block the other team's pushers. The ball vibrated and lit up with each hit so it was almost like the noise from an old pinball machine. The ball moved like crazy because any unbalanced force made it move quickly in that direction.

It took Mary about five minutes to get bored with the game.

Suzie had picked up on this by now. "You guys are not super sports fans so let's go get a massage at the Greek resort."

By now most of the flock had wandered off and gotten involved in discussions. Suzie had the duty to tour Joe and Mary around so the three of them flew off toward a lake in the distance. At the end of the lake was a huge spa with Greek influenced architecture.

"Watch this," Suzie said as they approached the lake. She zoomed down and grabbed a handful of water and threw it into the air. The droplets all formed together in the air, forming a perfect sphere that slowly dropped down in to the lake. Mary laughed and reached down to do it a few times herself.

The resort was astounding. On the outside were huge Greek columns two stories tall, sculpted like women.

"It's modeled after the Ancient Greek Caryatid Porch of the Erechtheion," Suzie informed them as they arrived. The floors were all magnetized so they could land and walk around.

There really wasn't any front door to the resort, they simply walked in. Once they stepped inside there were a lot of Doric, Ionic and Corinthian columns used to section off the different treatments you could get. At the entrance to each area was a beautiful sculpture of some Greek god like Zeus, holding a sign that said *The Baths, Massage*, etc. As you approached any treatment area, someone was notified and came out to help you. Beautiful and very relaxing harp music was playing and the acoustics in the building were perfect. Mary could not tell where the sound was coming from. It made for great background music but the sound was low enough that they could talk in a normal voice and not be interrupted by the music.

"Let's go do a massage," said Suzie.

"Ok," both Mary and Joe said in a kind of dumbfounded way, because they were awestruck at all the architecture, sculptures and frescos.

As they approached the massage area, a woman in a Greek robe walked out. "Hi," she said. "I am Adelphe, and I am so happy you decided to get massaged. It's great for your soul and good for your health. I know the guy Suzie likes to use. Should we have a woman for Joe and a man for Mary?"

Joe perked up a little when she said "woman for Joe" and suddenly got a little flustered when she said "a man for Mary." Mary knew Joe so well she picked up on it right away.

"It's OK, big boy," said Mary as she slapped Joe on the ass. "You can handle it."

"Well…..all right," said Joe.

"You guys are new here, aren't you?" said Adelphe.

"Yeah," said Joe. "We just came over from ISS, and we'll be going back shortly."

By this time they had walked back to a room with beautiful frescoes on the wall, and a man and woman in togas joined them. The room was open to the sky and there was sunlight everywhere. It was kind of like they were in an enclosed private courtyard on a nice summer day with the sunlight at the perfect temperature.

"Well," said Adelphe, "this might be a little unusual for you but I guarantee you will like it. Ambrosia here will work on Joe, and Aitalas will work on Mary. I am going to go gossip and work on Suzie and I will see you later."

"We are going to work on both of you in the same room," said Aitalas in a very pleasant but manly voice, "so the first thing is to change clothes. Here is a jockstrap for Joe and bikini for Mary. There is a vanity wall over there so why don't you go ahead and change now."

Joe and Mary looked at the clothes. The jock was real cute and had the Greek-looking logo for the resort right over the front of the jock and there were also logos all over Mary's bikini.

When Joe and Mary were finished changing and came out, several WorkerBots floated in the room and they had two wide and long tubes between them and the tubes had been commanded to be stationary. A bot came over to Joe and Mary so they had something to hang onto and it floated them across the room to the tubes.

"Let's get started," Aitalas said with a smile. "This is what we call the washing machine. You can see that the tube is obviously long enough and wide enough to easily accommodate your body. So I have opened a hatch at one end of the tube. You slide in and up to the other end so your head comes just outside the tube at the other end. Then I put a towel around your neck so the water does not get out and I close the hatch at the other end. Then we turn on jets of water, which will pulsate and go up and down your body from all angles. Let's try that out and see how you like it."

"Wow," said Mary, excited to try it.

The music in the room had been harp-like music but increased to a more up-tempo sound. Joe and Mary slid into the tubes and when their heads came out the other end, a towel was put around their neck in a way that prevented any water from coming out. Then they turned on the water jets.

"How does that feel?" Ambrosia asked Joe. "The temperature should be just right but I can change it."

"Ohhhh yeah," said Joe, obviously in heaven and almost nodding off.

"Let's change gears," said Aitalas.

Both Aitalas and Ambrosia touched some buttons and the jets accelerated, giving Mary the most amazing water massage she'd ever had in her life.

The treatment went on for about ten minutes, and when it was done, all the water was sucked down the tube and the machine softly dried them with warm air. When they came out of the tube, more bots entered the room and massaged them from all angles while making sure to keep them afloat in the air.

"Wow," Mary said dreamily. "I never even dreamed of a 360-degree massage. It feels amazing."

"Yeah," said Aitalas with a quick grin. "Just tell me what you like, and we can increase the pressure or lower it and go slower or faster."

"It tickles and feels good at the same time," Mary said as one of the bots reached a particularly ticklish spot.

"It seems like the bots do everything," said Joe.

"Yeah," said Ambrosia. "We have the robots doing almost everything for us. They can give you just the right amount of pressure and do it better than humans. But it is good to have humans around to participate in the massage. We are basically here for good vibes and conversation."

"I noticed that," said Joe. "We thought we had a lot of WorkerBots on Earth. You guys have really outdone us."

"It's easier here," said Aitalas, "We have almost no gravity so they can do almost everything you can dream of and there is not as much of a need for FixItBots because there is not as much wear and tear on machinery."

As they talked, the bots massaged their bodies with oils, which had a great warm penetrating feeling. The fragrance was really nice too. The WorkerBots were careful to suck up any stray drops that got loose and started floating about. After the massage, the bots put them back in the washing machine to wash off the oils. Mary decided to start a discussion about the fate of L5P because that was what they were here for.

"What do you think about ISS taking over L5P?" she asked their masseuses.

"Typical politicians," said Aitalas. "They want to save us from ourselves. What that really means is that they think we are not behaving in the way they want us to. It's the same old story with most leaders throughout history. Politicians first argue that they needed to strongly control the people because there are limited supplies and with their superior wisdom they are best ones to decide who should get what. Now that we have solved most of our basic needs with WorkerBots and Replicators, the politicians have to have another excuse to dominate and control their fellow humans so in this case they say we are immoral, endangering unsuspecting humans and therefore L5P needs to be reined in so they can control it. Who are they to judge? We are just following where evolution wants to naturally take us."

"But there are extremes," said Joe. "Don't you think there is something wrong with allowing people to talk other people into allowing the human body to morph into a blob of jelly?"

"That's a big question," said Aitalas. "We argue about that all the time here. People have died by going to absolute zero G and doing no exercise to keep muscle tone because it is too much of a shock to the system. But the people who want that say we can gradually trend in that direction and the body will morph and adapt. As far as destroying bodies is concerned, look back in the history books on Earth where there were times when people would engage in sporting contests where the whole idea was for your opponent to intentionally damage your body and vice versa. Did we stop them? No, we paid them some of the highest wages in our society. Go figure that one out."

"Yes," Mary said, "but this is different. You are changing the entire human body for generations to come."

"You are right," said Aitalas, "but did you ever consider that perhaps the lives created at L5P may be superior to the life forms on Earth? Why should we let the government say we can't be allowed to progress and evolve to a better life form?

We choose to be what we are by our own free will. We are not harming the government, so why should the government harm us? The duty of the government is to protect our freedom and allow us to make the choices we want to make and that includes evolving however we want to – even if some people don't like it. Does the government think they are god? I think I am a better god than they are! "

Right about then Suzie walked into the room and she was totally content.

"God, that was really good!" Suzie said, "I do this once a week and I love it! Hey, we gotta go. I am sure you are tired by now so let's get a little sleep and then we can go see Amy. Do you want to stay at my place or go back to Jack's?"

"Let's stay at your place!" said Mary because she was dying to see how people lived at L5P. They were ready to say good-bye and leave the resort.

Chapter 9

Home at L5P

Joe and Mary were tired and happy to go to Suzie's house. The massage was great but when it was done, it left them feeling so pleasantly relaxed that all they wanted to do was sleep.

As Joe, Mary, and Suzie left the resort, everyone escorted them to the door with a lot of good wishes. Payment was handled just as it was on Earth. The minute they'd entered the establishment, the payment info from their SavvyCams had been recognized by the spa, so their accounts were automatically charged for the treatments they'd received. No need for any physical transaction.

Mary knew her own account must be getting low, because the Technology Dividends didn't allow for a lot of luxuries. That was why people need to do projects. The extra money they earned for this project would keep them in luxuries for a while, which would be nice. Plus, it just gave them something interesting to do.

They took off and started flying for a nearby mountain. As they approached it, they got a strong updraft, which felt incredible, and allowed them to just glide right over the mountain.

The homes up here were separated by a good distance and had real nice landscapes with lots of flowers and plants. Suzie's entrance patio was sort of like Jack's and overlooked the valley. There were no guard rails, which made the space seem very expansive, lots of room for people to land and take off

As they landed, the doors opened and Suzie led them into her dome house. A man was standing there with his back to them, watching a ticker tape of stocks and figures run across the screen. The screen ate up about one-third of the wall and several of his friends were on the screen in discussion with him. Another third of the wall showed people engaging in political discussions. He was having a somewhat "friendly angry" talk with one of them. When the patio door opened an alert went up on the screen. He quickly turned around and smiled as he cut off the conversation.

"This is my husband, Bill," said Suzie. "He is into stocks, planet exploration, and math – not my cup of tea but I love to hear him talk about it."

"Hi," said Bill as he gave a hearty hand shake to both Mary and Joe.

"I see you are into stocks," said Joe.

"Yeah," said Bill. "It does two things for me. First, it gives me a real good understanding about what is happening in society, and second, it gives me a chance to make some money. Right now, I am a little mad because Zork Inc. led everyone to believe they were doing really well, and just now they delivered a bad report – it caused me to lose money but I am diversified so it is not too bad. It still makes me mad, and I was going over that with my friends in a little investment club we have."

"You are into space travel too?" asked Mary, as Suzie gestured for them to get comfortable and make themselves at home. "What are the big happenings in space travel?"

"Well," said Bill, obviously happy to have a chance to talk about one of his passions. "A lot of people are working on having an artificial miniature sun for L5P. If we can get it worked out right, it would allow us to drift off into space to go anywhere we wanted to. It could be interplanetary, interstellar, or even intergalactic space. That would solve a lot of the political issues but there are big arguments against moving L5P because we feel tied to Earth, even though we will never go there again. It's hard to tell what will happen."

"I'm going to give Mary and Joe the guest room," said Suzie

"Yeah," said Bill. "I think we have two NetBeds there."

"We prefer one," said Mary

"You sure?" said Suzie, with a mysterious grin. "OK. Let's set up one sleep space."

"I think it's cool that you have social groups up here," said Joe

"Yeah," said Bill, "it is just like Earth. We have different groups you like to belong to and you go to meetings in your dome with them. Usually we just talk about the news and what is happening but sometimes something interesting comes up and we physically fly out and get together. Overall it is pretty much like Earth. You get enough money from the Technology Dividend to just get by, but if you want to have more money you join a project and get involved or you can start your own project or business and sometimes do real well. So there is a safety net for everyone but encouragement to get out and make something happen."

"Yeah," said Suzy. "I like to volunteer sometimes too. I fly around with my friends to see who we can help out. Like today, we followed the ambulance and found you."

"Do you have a room where I can do some work?" Joe asked.

"Sure," said Suzy, "the first door on the right. It has all the standard dome controls, just like on Earth."

Joe and Mary walked down the hall into the room. As they entered, it lit up and the background graphics on the dome were like they were on a hillside on Earth on a sunny day.

"Dome, call Sam." said Joe

The dome knew from Joe's cell phone who Sam was. The default on domes was to give you about one third of the dome for your viewing screen. A clock with moving hands appeared on the screen and the dialing sound echoed through the room as the computer tried to get through to Earth. Communication with L5P was difficult but you could dial out if you had a government pass and ID, which Sam put on their SavvyCams. There was a little fuzz, and then Sam came on the screen.

"Hi, Sam," said Joe and Mary together

"Hi, you guys," said Sam. "I am getting all your feeds but have you had any luck in getting a meeting with Dylan Thomas?"

"Not yet," said Joe, "but we talk to Amy again tomorrow and hopefully she can arrange it, because she really seems to be the only contact here to get to him."

"There is a big problem," said Sam. "It is not public knowledge yet, and I don't want you to tell anyone, but Bruno has managed to get a hearing tomorrow with the ISS directors. If there is no testimony from Dylan Thomas, who, I might add, has never agreed to talk to the directors at all, then they will vote to bring L5Pilgrim back under ISS control and start to reverse all that has happened there. They want to slowly speed the station back up and have an army of medical people around to help transition people back to normal humans."

"That's a problem," said Joe. "L5Pilgrim does not want to change. If you force the change, it will probably lead to lots of physical damage to the people here and probably a lot of deaths, because they have completely adjusted to this environment."

"You have a point," said Sam, "but they want to hear Dylan Thomas defend his colony and what is happening to the people there. If he can't defend his position, then they feel it is obvious that the bad things people say is happening there is true and therefore the ISS needs to step in to save the loss of any more human lives. Unfortunately, time has run out for us. If you can't get me testimony tomorrow, then it's over for L5Pilgrim. Bruno Nightfire will be considered a hero. He will also be taking the project job I wanted to give to you."

"I don't feel so bad about losing the job," said Joe, "but I hate to see this community destroyed."

"These people really seem to have a great thing going on," Mary added. "Everyone is very happy with the way things are. I don't see how anyone else has the right to tell them what to do. Especially if they've never been up here to see what the truth is."

"Sorry," said Sam, "but they have just as strong an argument – they feel lives are being brainwashed and destroyed by converting the people of L5P into creatures who can never walk the Earth again. They say it is a lesson people need to learn – you cannot abuse your fellow humans. Not all stories have a happy ending. I will use whatever feed you send. I gotta go now."

Joe and Mary really felt let down as they walked back to find Suzie and Bill who were now in a small social dome room which was all lit up for a virtual party. Bill and Suzie were all happy and laughing, talking to their friends. It was social hour and a good 50 or so people were on the 360-degree screen. It was just as though you were at a real party with small groups of people all over the place talking to each other but it was a virtual get together.

"Joe, Mary," said Suzie with excitement. "Come over here and get near me. I am standing on the WalkPad."

WalkPads were used to move around a social room. It was just a 360-degree treadmill that was very sensitive to your feet.

Joe and Mary came over and stood by Suzie.

"Let's go meet George and Barbara," said Suzie. "They are into politics, and you seem to want to go down that road."

Suzie walked to the right and the entire dome image moved with her, just like they were walking around a room. She walked past a few people to a group of four people.

"Hey, George and Barb," said Suzie, "this is Joe and Mary. They are going back to Earth tomorrow, and they want to be journalists so L5P is the first story they were given to cover."

"Hey," said George, "that's great."

"I hope you say something nice," giggled Barb. "We don't want to be anyone's enemy."

"I am sure you must know," said Mary, "that ISS is real disturbed about L5P. They think you are some kind of runaway colony."

"Yeah," said George with a smile. "That's about right. We are a runaway colony and damn, we are having a great time doing it! We all discussed the whole issue forever and we finally voted on it and we decided collectively to slow down the wheel and float free. We offered anyone who wanted to leave the right to leave. In fact, we begged people to leave. We have all the civil rights anyone has on ISS. So what's the problem?"

"Well," said Mary. "They say that you are kind of like a cult or an extreme religious group or something. You brainwash people and once they have been here for a while they can't go back to Earth."

"I'm glad you put it that way," said George, "Let's go with that. Suppose somebody gets all wrapped up in religion X. In fact, they get so wrapped up that they wind up in an almost monk-like existence living in the temple of religion X. Now you could argue that they are a little brainwashed or that their life is wasted because they could have become a productive member of society. But we don't do that, do we? I mean as long as you don't get so crazy that you go around killing innocent people, we are happy with that, aren't we? In fact, religion X probably gives good values to the person's life. So we at L5P are like that, except we kind of worship freedom and the ability to live in almost zero G. We are good people and happy people in our beliefs, so what is wrong with that?'

"Well," said Joe, "the argument is that you can always save the person who gets too carried away with religion X, but once you change your body, you can't go back and you can't be saved."

"Let's see," said George. "Who gets to decide which religion is a good one and which one is a bad one? They are all good in their own way, so why should the government be allowed to decide this one is bad and this one is good? I understand your concern about changing your body but don't you understand that you have to allow people the right to exercise their free will even if you don't like what they want to do? If you want to jump off the side of a cliff and parachute, I think you are absolutely crazy and you could damage your body horribly, but I don't put you in jail and try to deprogram you. I allow you to express your free will however you want."

"You are creating a new species," said Joe. "You won't be able to walk the Earth again. Doesn't that bother you?"

"You got it wrong," said Geroge. "Joe and Mary, you will not be able to live here and enjoy our wonderful life because you have chosen to be shackled to the Earth and a slave to gravity. Your joints will wear out much faster than ours and your whole life in general will be a lot worse than ours. Doesn't that bother you?"

"I don't know," said Mary. "Maybe it is OK, but it is really weird and some people turn their bodies into blobs of jelly and die."

"It is evolution on the fast track," said George. "We don't know where it is going to take us but we feel it's going in the direction that feels right to us. Personally, I don't feel I want to push the envelope any further. I love it right where I am, but there are some people who want to go absolutely zero G and some of them have died because of it. Who knows where we will go?"

Mary was starting to yawn a little.

"Let's go to bed," said Suzie, noticing how tired they were.

"OK," both Joe and Mary said, and everyone said good-night to each other.

They walked out of the main dome and down the hall to the guest room. By the time they got to the room, a WorkerBot had a NetBed set up. It was a large cage-like structure made of a tightly woven ropelike substance that was very elastic so you would bounce off the walls and the whole thing was suspended in mid-air. There was a closet for their clothes in the room and real soothing harp-like music was playing.

"The bots will wake you in about six hours," said Suzie. "We don't need too much sleep up here because we don't do that much work. The door to the NetBed is the red end."

"OK," said Mary, "see you soon."

Joe and Mary were both pretty exhausted because of all the changes their bodies had gone through and the massage on top of that. They thought they would fall asleep in a heartbeat. They took their clothes off and climbed into the NetBed and almost immediately went to sleep.

Then it happened. On Earth, you roll over and put your arms around your loved one and it was all peaceful and tranquil, but floating in space your arms and legs are all over the place and when you are asleep, you don't know where they are going.

So Joe woke up as Mary's elbow bonked him in the head, and Mary woke up with Joe crashing in to her side after he bounced off the wall. Finally, they both woke up with their arms and feet all tangled together in some weird twisted manner.

"Owww," said Mary as she shook Joe to get him fully awake. "That hurt."

"Huh?" said Joe groggily. "What hurt who?"

"That does it," said Mary. "WorkerBot, we want two Net-Beds."

Almost immediately, the door opened and a WorkerBot brought in another NetBed.

A soft voice said, *"Suzie left instructions to have a second NetBed ready to be brought in."*

They both laughed and separated into the two NetBeds.

Chapter 10

Dylan Thomas

After six hours of sleep, some nice soft French horns began to play softly, slowing waking Joe and Mary up.

They put their AstroSuits on, said goodbye to Suzie with hugs and kisses, and went to Jack's place. As they approached, they saw Amy floating in the air just outside of his deck.

Joe and Mary zoomed toward Amy, then flipped head over heels and did a perfect midair stop right in front of Amy with big smiles on their face and laughter. Mary was actually really starting to love the freedom the AstroSuits provided. Better than a NutriSuit anyday.

"Wow," said Amy, "you guys learn fast. You are pretty good at that."

Jack came out and said, "OK, I need the suits back. Larry just arrived with the cargo ship."

"Wait," said Mary, feeling like things were moving much too fast. "We still have important business to do. We need our interview." They'd had a good time up here, but they still really hadn't accomplished anything.

"Go ahead and change," said Amy "and I will meet you at the L5P portal where we first met, then we will talk about it."

Joe and Mary were a little confused but went along with it. After all, they were guests here.

After changing clothes, two WorkerBots appeared to help them get to Amy. Joe and Mary sat on them like they were riding a horse and they went off to meet Amy.

As they were traveling, Joe and Mary got a message from Sam. He said that Bruno had managed to get the decision hearing pushed up on an emergency basis and they were going to meet in about five minutes.

Then they arrived at the L5P portal.

"Amy," Joe said as soon as they saw her, "we have a real crisis here, and I don't think you know how bad it really is. We absolutely have to talk to Dylan Thomas immediately, and I mean within the next five minutes. Can you take us to him now? The fate of L5P is hanging in the balance."

"No," said Amy. "He wants to be kept out of politics at all costs and, to be honest, your visit is starting to get too political." She gave them a suspicious look. "WorkerBot, block phones. Sorry, but I have just cut off your phones and it is time to go. Your phones will be restored after you leave L5Pilgrim."

"Amy," said Mary, "there are some really horrible decisions that are being made right now. If we don't get testament from Dylan Thomas right now, the entire L5Pilgrim world will come to an end. It is that important. I wouldn't say this if it wasn't true."

Amy just stared at Joe and Mary and did nothing.

"OK," Joe said, "I swore I would not talk about this but I just can't let all these lives and the whole L5Pilgrim community be lost. There is a guy named Bruno Nightfire who is in charge of security at ISS and he is having an emergency ISS board meeting right now to vote to shut down L5Pilgrim right at this very moment. It will happen immediately once the vote is taken. Your only hope is to have Dylan Thomas give testimony as to why L5P should be left alone and the board will only listen to Dylan Thomas."

"I am sure you have been around for a while," said Amy, "and I am sure you have heard the argument for L5P from everyone. We all want things just as they are. Listen, nobody has the right to subjugate people and kill their freedom. It is something you are born with and something you have a right to. When you kill freedom, you kill the spirit of the whole human race."

"Bruno will take over L5P with his security forces and destroy what you have built," Joe warned, frustrated by Amy's lack of action. "Gravity will be brought back and lots of lives could be lost. It will be a gruesome end to everything everyone here has worked for."

"Let me tell you something about Bruno Nightfire," said Amy. "Bruno was among us for a short time and he actually wanted to live here. He said he was invaluable to L5P because he was an important official at ISS and he could guarantee our freedom. He pointed out that he even has the right office at ISS because he oversees security and this would allow him to stand up for our rights. Unfortunately Bruno also wanted to form a very strong police force, the L5P security force, which only he would be in charge of and wanted lots of other dictatorial powers over us. Then he started talking really crazy ideas about how L5P could become the home for something called the Avatar Initiative and fill the place with what sounded like robots that were clones of humans. We rejected it. We don't need a pharaoh or dictator running our lives at his whim and we really don't want to evolve into robots."

Mary shook her head as she listened. Well, that explained a lot!

"There is an old saying," Amy continued. "'If we restrict liberty to attain security we will lose them both.' We could see what was coming our way, and we did not want to go down the road Bruno wanted to take us and we asked him to leave. We had the WorkerBots put him on the next cargo ship out of here and we decertified his ID. We immediately elected Dylan Thomas as our leader and protected him from ISS management. So it doesn't surprise me that Bruno would find another way to try and forcibly take over L5Pilgrim."

"But we have to speak to Dylan Thomas," Joe said. "He is the only legitimate voice of L5Pilgrim, and we only have minutes to do this. He needs to tell them what happened, why they shouldn't listen to Bruno. Without his testimony, ISS will shut L5P down."

"No!" said Amy. "Don't you understand? They just want Dylan Thomas out in the open so they can target him. They will arrest him for some stupid reason and then move in on us. Don't you understand what is happening here? This is all politics and almost all politicians want nothing more than more power and more power. They have already decided our fate one way or another, and there is nothing we can do about it."

"It's really important," said Mary, who now was starting to get tears in her eyes. These people and their plight had become very important to her in the short time she'd been here.

"No," said Amy. "I know that is what Dylan feels, and I don't want put his life on the line and destroy him for nothing."

"WorkerBots," said Amy, "take Joe and Mary to Larry."

The WorketBots started to drift away with Joe and Mary, signaling an end to the conversation.

Mary was now totally overcome with tears and started to sob.

"You have no right to doom the L5Pilgrims!" Mary shouted loudly and sobbed in a hysterical voice, "Time has run out! I don't care who loses their life or what it costs. Why won't you let us speak to him! Damn you! You can't do this! How can you speak for Dylan Thomas?"

Amy looked at Joe and Mary with a helpless look.

"Because I *am* Dylan Thomas," said Amy.

With that, the bots drifted away with Joe and Mary.

Chapter 11

Home Again

As Mary and Joe boarded Larry's ship, Mary couldn't stop crying. She was distraught over the whole experience. Joe held her in his arms and quietly murmured comforting words in her ears, but it didn't help. She felt so sad that the community would be destroyed and replaced by something much worse. It was the freedom and liberty of the human soul being destroyed by those who want dictatorships and the conversion of humans to machines…and it was all over now.

They just left their phones off and asked Larry to immediately transfer them to the next shuttle to Earth.

Not every story has a happy ending and they say time heals all wounds, but Joe and Mary were really hurt and couldn't help feeling like they'd failed. They shut off all communication on anything around them and made the trip home in silence. There was really nothing left to say. ISS was going to destroy all those happy, flying people on L5P and there was nothing they could do about it now.

Eventually they got to Earth and walked out of the Space-Port to their waiting BubbleVan.

The van pulled out and headed for home. As they were getting close to home, the screen in the van started blinking the emergency alert message sign. You could shut down your communication devices but there was always a way for people to reach you in an extreme emergency. Everyone knew not to use the signal unless it was extremely urgent.

Mary and Joe ignored it for a while, but it kept flashing.

"I guess we're going to have to answer eventually," Mary finally said and the screen opened up. She was terrified some-one was going to tell them that the worst had happened on L5P.

"Damn!" said Sam, when his face appeared on the screen. "You guys are impossible to reach. Did you hear the news?"

"What news?" they both said in unison.

"I can't believe you guys went all the way home and you haven't even been watching the news," said Sam. "Here, I will play it for you."

A video of the live telecast of the board of directors meet-ing at ISS popped up.

Bruno had just finished up his case. "*So I urge a vote now on restoring L5Pilgrim to a normal station like ISS. I know some people may be damaged and some may even be killed in the process, but we have to act now or the situation will ex-plode with all the new applicants. It will endanger the whole human species if we do not stop it now.*"

The director said, "*I have just been notified that the direc-tor of the Journalism Project on Earth has turned in testimony for numerous citizens of L5P. There is an emergency live feed he wants us to see. You make a good case, Bruno, but let's just listen to the live feed from the L5P portal and then vote."*

The screen lit up with a live feed from the L5Pilgrim portal used to converse with Amy for interviews with ISS. From this angle, you could easily see Amy, Joe and Mary. The live feed started right where Joe and Mary started having the confrontation with Amy.

As soon as the feed started, Bruno immediately stood up in protest.

"This has to stop," said Bruno. *"The laws clearly state that only the leader of L5Pilgrim, Dylan Thomas, is allowed to speak for L5P and—"*

Bruno did not get to go any further because as soon as he started to speak the director of the board held his hand up with his palm toward Bruno the way you tell a dog to stop and sternly waved his hand down, meaning Bruno better shut up and be seated or action would be taken.

When Amy started relating her history with Bruno, everyone on the board turned and looked at Bruno with eyes that said, "You never told us that….how could you do that?"

Finally, just after Amy said she was Dylan Thomas, the director turned off the feed.

"Well," the director said. *"It appears Mr. Nightfire has been less than honest with the board about his past and it also appears from all the polls that the citizens of L5Pilgrim do want the society that they have. As director, I ask the board to vote now on the following two items. We hereby dismiss Bruno Nightfire from his position and order him sent back to Earth never to return to ISS again and Ms. Amy Worthington is hereby appointed to the new position of director of L5Pilgrim with all the rights to determine their own fate that ISS has for itself.*

All those in favor, please raise your hand and say aye."

The entire board except Bruno raised their hand and said "Aye" in unison.

Then the video ended, and Sam was back on the screen.

"That was a worldwide telecast," Sam said, "and you obviously got the job as journalist if you want it, Joe. So you got lucky on this one." Then the screen went black.

Mary and Joe turned to each other in shock, then hugged each other ecstatically. "I forgot he was finding a way to access the portal at L5P and it came just in time," Mary cried. "I didn't think we had a chance."

"I can't believe we did it," Joe told her, then hugged her passionately.

Shortly after that, the van pulled up in front of the Davis house. As the van doors opened, Bobby and Daisy were pretending to fly in front of the house.

Bobby had already had the replicator create AstroSuits, complete with wings and tails, for him and Daisy.

Bobby and Daisy did an imaginary flight over to Joe and Mary. Bobby opened his arms to make sure Joe and Mary could admire his full AstroSuit.

Bobby also had a huge nametag printed on his chest that said *Dylan Thomas*. Daisy was standing next to him with wings up and hers said *Amy Worthington*.

"We want to be free," said Daisy. "We like to fly. We can go anywhere. We are our future. We have to go back to the KiddieDome."

A WorkerBot was doing the lawn nearby and Joe called it over. He picked Bobby up and had him stand on the Worker-

Bot so Bobby was a little higher than Joe.

"I told you," said Joe with pride, "that I would have a little poem for you when I got back, so I made a little poem up just for you, Mr. Robert Davis. It is called *Master Robert* and it goes like this:

For people to come and changes we make
For the new species created - that regenerate
For things we will do that we cannot retake
There's a question to ask which we cannot mistake

We're designed to evolve and we cast with it our fate
Changing our bodies into a whole different state
Will we become gears made to function much faster
Or will we evolve with evolution as master?

For each living soul their body will rust
It's ashes to ashes and it's dust to dust,
The clock it is ticking and decisions we must
But which path will we take and who will we trust?

Now it's your turn to take charge moving faster
And choose how you will help to avoid a disaster
When time takes its toll, your choices harden into plaster
What will you have done, young Robert, young master?